THE OFFICIAL NOVELIZATION

MARTYRS

WRITTEN BY

CHRISTIAN FRANCIS

BASED ON THE SCREENPLAY BY

PASCAL LAUGIER

ECHO ON PUBLISHING

CHAPTER ONE

SLAUGHTERHOUSE

The viewfinder brightened as the Super 8 camera whirred to life.

As the gears clacked in their mechanical rhythm, the image flickered as the exposure searched for its balance. Whiteness bloomed before soon settling into the burned orange glow of the afternoon it was filming.

Doctor Emmanuel Coisson, in his sixties, stood at the side of a country lane. Wearing a tweed coat and large horn-rimmed glasses, he held a small microphone as he looked into the lens, its cord running out of the frame. The wind muffled his voice into incoherence when he tried to speak.

"Move a bit to the right," the cameraman's voice called out. "Got too much interference, I can't hear you."

The man turned his shoulder against the breeze, "How about now?" he asked in his maudlin tone into the microphone.

"Much better," the cameraman answered. "Start whenever you want."

The doctor nodded. "Good." He looked back into the camera and addressed his audience. "We're on the D-107, at marker one-two-eight. Mirepoix lies seven kilometers south, Chamfors north. It was here, on this stretch of rural wasteland, that the child in question was found."

As he pointed off to the right, the camera jolted, shifting to follow.

"She was found right there," the doctor continued. "Beside this old sign."

An old billboard stood on the verge, its metal frame covered in rust, with its display long worn of the advertisement it once carried. Vines climbed from the base and wrapped around until they swallowed most of the sign.

The film cut abruptly with a pop of light and a click in the sound.

It resumed instantly, with the doctor now walking down the road, the camera beside him, filming him intently as he spoke.

"She'd been running barefoot for quite some time, sustaining multiple lacerations on her plantar surfaces. It was just before eleven p.m. that a truck driver found her back there. He stated that she threw herself into his arms, crying about what had happened to her, but soon after, she stopped speaking altogether. As the shock wore off, she mentally shut herself away."

He paused, looking past the camera toward the empty stretch of road ahead.

"Where she was held," he spoke in an almost bored tone. "That is less than three kilometers from here."

The wind rose against the microphone again, swallowing his last words, as the camera followed his gaze down the road.

The footage cut to the base of a large, abandoned industrial structure, comprising three separate buildings. The doctor walked over the weed and bramble overgrowth, across the yard, leading up to a doorless entrance.

The whole front of this monolithic structure had been left to ruin, with countless graffiti tags from the years sprayed over its decaying shell.

"This was the Chamfors slaughterhouse, until 1963 when its owners were forced to shut down because of what was called unclean practices... The governmental report stated that they'd been processing carcasses that had already begun to decay, washing off mold and rot in vinegar before sending them to market."

He pointed to the smashed windows on a higher floor. "Since then, vandals have left their marks, but this place is too far from metropolitan life to attract many squatters. There's nothing around here apart from fallow fields and woodland."

He walked to the open doorway. "This is building B."

As the cameraman followed him inside, the

darkness blotted out the viewfinder until a snap of a button echoed, and a camera-mounted light illuminated the small corridor around them.

A dampness clung to the concrete and tiled walls as the doctor strode ahead, knowing where he was going, using the light behind him to step over fallen brickwork and remnants of smashed furniture. He spoke loudly as he walked.

"Watch your step, there's junk all over the floor."

The warning came a bit late, as the cameraman stumbled over a large piece of concrete that had fallen away from the wall.

The doctor continued. "Lucie Jurin was reported missing on October 16th last year, and was found three weeks ago, one year and nine days after her disappearance. 25th October 1971." He stopped to look back at the camera. "This slaughterhouse was discovered shortly afterwards by the investigators from the gendarmerie unit out of Bressan-Lamorie."

Turning to his left, he motioned to a half-closed door leading to a dark room.

"She was locked in here," he said, pushing open the door to let the camera go in first. "Try not to breathe too deeply," he added.

The white light from the camera picked up the filthy, small cell, where, in the corner, lay a mattress. One stained with blood, muck, and excretion.

The cameraman coughed as the stench of old decay hit his throat.

The doctor spoke from behind. "She lived here for

a long time, no covers, no comfort, using a bucket for a toilet."

The camera turned. The bucket was still there, still beside the mattress, still crusted with filth.

The light then turned and fell upon the decayed remains of something. An unidentifiable matter coated the stone floor.

"What you are looking at is what the investigators surmised was her food. They believed that her captors fed her spoiled meat and rotten vegetables, which they threw onto the floor for her to eat from."

The lens rose, shaking slightly in the cameraman's anxious grip. There, another element within the room came into view: butcher hooks dangling on chains from the ceiling.

The doctor kept talking as the camera drifted around the room, filming every corner and item.

"They found her hair, pieces of fingernails. Clawed into the wall as she tried to escape time and time again." His words came out cold, devoid of emotion, as if he were reading from a scientific journal. "She wasn't raped, that's for sure. The medical examination proved that she was still a virgin. But it was the rest of her body that was damaged... she was repeatedly beaten."

The camera stopped filming the room and rested on the doctor once more.

"When she was found, her injuries corresponded to extreme abuse. She had a large hematoma above her left eyebrow. She was suffering severe malnutrition, dehydration, and mild hypothermia." His clinical tone made the horror of this room somehow worse.

"Come with me," he said, walking over to an adjacent room.

In the middle of the room was a tall metallic chair, with clamps on the armrest and legs, as well as a perforated seat.

"The seat allows the person sitting upon it to relieve themselves. You just put the bucket underneath. Which is what they did."

"Jesus," the cameraman gasped, to which the doctor shot him an unapproving glare.

Ignoring his disdain at the interruption, he continued. "Lucie must have spent days on this chair. The investigators found traces of her blood all over and around it from months of battery and torture."

The camera circled the metal device, filming it from every angle, with its light picking up the black stains of blood spattered around the floor.

"She had infections from the cuffs on her wrists, showing the extent of how often she was restrained." The doctor had the camera's attention again. "It is worth noting that this was all during her growth phase. At 10 years old, Lucie's muscular system and skeleton reacted well despite everything she was subjected to."

The cameraman couldn't help but ask a question, though he was not supposed to speak. "H—How did she get out of here?" he said, sounding as if he was about to vomit.

The doctor stared at him for a second before

shrugging. "Lucie didn't talk about what happened. So we simply don't know."

"But, who would do something like this?"

The doctor looked into the lens with a doubtful grimace.

A cloud of static cut off the footage, buzzing loudly for a while until starting up again. The Chamfors slaughterhouse was gone, the room where the atrocities happened now replaced by the outside of a small rehabilitation center.

When the picture returned, the shot was from across a lawn, filming Doctor Coisson, who was now dressed in a white lab coat, sitting on a small bench beside a small girl.

With a comforting smile, the doctor spoke to her as she stared blankly at the grass, silent.

The camera zoomed in to get a clearer shot, and the extent of her injuries came into focus. She was so thin that her muscles were barely visible, and her skin just looked as if it were wrapped tight around her small frame. With a large bandage over her left eye, the other one stared with a haunted and frightened look. Her skin, though pale, was littered with fading bruises. Her cracked lips and dark bags under her eyes betrayed the heavy medication trying to take hold of her. Her hair, cut choppily short and without care, reinforced her sickly appearance.

It was obvious who this was. Lucie Jurin. The subject of the abuse from the slaughterhouse.

Behind the bench, as the doctor continued talking to her, a nun stood attentively by.

The shot quickly cut to another part of the grounds, to the rose garden, where Lucie was hobbling painfully with the help of a walker. Each step on her bandaged feet hurt her, and she winced in agony every time. The doctor stood by, urging her to continue. Nothing that was said could be heard, but the nun who followed behind didn't look happy with what was happening.

As the pain in Lucie's head got too much, she collapsed onto the gravel, and the camera was immediately switched off.

It came back to life in an exercise room. Filled with parallel bars, exercise mats, and a small hydrotherapy pool, Lucie was sitting in a chair opposite Dr. Coisson's desk.

She still had no words to speak. Her eyes fluttered, trying to keep awake, slumped with her arms on her knees. The melancholy she carried was heartbreaking to witness.

The person who watched this video picked up the remote and switched the television off.

"Such a pity," came the old female voice.

CHAPTER TWO
REHABILITATION

Four months passed at the St Denys Children's Rehabilitation Center, and Lucie Jurin was a few days away from her eleventh birthday.

Ever since *Le Monde* splashed her school photo across its front page with the headline "FOUND!", the press from all over the country had been stalking the center like vultures. Camping in the car park, crowding the entrance, hoping to see any sign of the kidnapped girl, and hoping to get an interview. Hoping to get a photo.

Today, though, was the first day that no journalists showed up outside. They had gotten nothing except speculation from all their weeks here, so had mutually decided that the story was no longer of interest to them.

Lucie knew nothing about this, as she had been hidden away behind the darkened glass of the center's windows, behind their high brick walls.

She had remained silent since she arrived, obediently doing what she was told. When she was not needed to do anything, she just sat in a chair in her room, doing nothing except existing in her own mind.

Her hair had started to grow out, and the staff had taken care to trim it properly, making her appear healthier and more cared for.

She still relied on a walker; her feet throbbed with the slow pain of healing. When she followed the nun to get her shower or went for her daily exercises, they always passed the television room, where the other young patients were. The familiar *clomp clomp* of her making her way down the corridor made them turn, and she met their curious gazes with an expressionless yet haunted gaze.

As the clock hit 8 p.m., with all exercise done for the day, the nun had led Lucie back to her room, holding open the door as she clomped inside.

Every evening was the same. As Lucie weakly stood there, she was undressed. Her body hunched and unable to stand straight for long. She was still so gaunt, but her bruises had mostly faded to a dull yellow across her porcelain pallor.

"Would you want the night light on?" the nun asked, picking up the nightgown and placing it carefully over Lucie's head.

The child sadly nodded, the only way she had communicated since being admitted here.

The bedroom door opened, and an older nun stepped inside. She was the facility's head nurse as well as the mother superior of the convent that cared for the patients.

"I have a surprise for you, Ms. Jurin," the mother superior said.

She was holding the hand of a small girl, around the same age as Lucie. The child had a large black eye, but her neat braids and rosy complexion made her look otherwise healthy. She smiled meekly.

The nun finished dressing Lucie and clasped her hands together at the sight of this new arrival.

"Well, this is a nice surprise, isn't it, Lucie?"

The mother superior bent down to the child next to her. "Anna, you'll be sharing the room for the next day or two, is that okay?"

Anna nodded.

"And this is Lucie. She is very shy. Much shyer than you, remember what I told you?"

"She doesn't talk?" Anna asked.

"Exactly," the mother superior nodded. "Now, Lucie? Are you okay with Anna staying here?" Without waiting for any reply, she nodded. "Good, now say hello." The mother superior let go of Anna's hand and gently pushed her into the room.

Anna took a few cautious steps forward and peered at Lucie. "Hello," she said, her voice as soft as a dormouse. "My name's Anna Assaoui."

Lucie didn't answer her, but instead just stared at the girl's bruised eye.

The mother superior glanced over to the nun. "Do

you have something for Anna to change into? Her things are not arriving until tomorrow."

With a nod, the nun walked over to the cupboard and brought out a pair of clean, white pajamas. Handing them to Anna, she motioned to the bathroom. "You can change in there, my dear."

The mother superior smiled as Anna shut the door.

"She's resourceful," she said, speaking as if Lucie was not standing there between them.

"Do you know her?" the nun asked.

The mother superior nodded. "From one of the other centers." She quickly lowered her voice. "Her mother has issues with alcohol, so she was placed with her uncle... But he was... a lot worse. He did that to her, and... Anyway, she's here now, and we shall be caring for her. On Monday, we can move both to the dormitory."

She noticed Lucie staring up at her, attentive to hearing Anna's story.

The mother superior's tone quickly changed. "She's very sweet, you'll see." She returned Lucie's gaze. "And you'll be just as sweet back, yes, Ms. Jurin?"

Lucie didn't reply.

The nun then guided the child over to her bed, leaving the walker by the dresser, with Lucie gripping onto her arm for support.

As she got under the covers and the nun tucked them over her, Lucie looked like a tiny, helpless animal in the large bed.

Anna soon came out of the bathroom in her pajamas.

"You can sleep there," the mother superior said, pointing to the empty bed on the other side of the room.

"Thank you," Anna replied politely.

Lucie kept staring at the girl without replying. But where the other children in the center felt uncomfortable when Lucie stared, Anna did not. She just held her gaze and smiled back.

"May our lord Jesus Christ watch over you both tonight," The mother superior said with a smile as the other nun joined her.

The main lights were off, the door was closed, and the night light glowed from the plug socket. In its orange light, Anna could not see Lucie clearly, but could sense that the girl was still staring over at her.

"Did someone hurt you too?" Anna asked.

From her bed, Lucie nodded, which Anna could just make out in the half-light.

"Who did it? Someone in your family?"

No reply came.

Soon, a thick silence fell over the room, and Anna turned onto her back, looking up at the darkened ceiling. She was not a girl haunted by suffering as Lucie was; instead, she carried a silent resignation for her lot in life. Accepting without dwelling on her hurt.

A rustling of bedsheets caught her attention. She looked back over and saw Lucie getting out of bed, with every movement strained and aching.

Anna watched silently as Lucie walked over to her frame and clomped her way over to the door. When she got there, she wedged the walker under the handle. Her method of blocking this entrance was clearly practiced, and something that Lucie did nightly.

Anna's eyes adjusted more to the dark as Lucie turned back with an unsteady gait.

"Are you scared?" Anna asked.

No answer.

"You can come here if you want?" Anna said, moving over. "The bed's big, and we'd be safer together, right?"

With a look of initial hesitation, Lucie cast a worried look back to her makeshift barricade, then hobbled back to her own bed, disappearing under the sheets.

Anna watched, disappointed, before lying back down.

———

In the rehabilitation center, days felt like hours as they drifted by without much difference. Mondays to Saturdays, the routine for each patient was the same, making the passage of time almost imperceptible. Awake at 7. Breakfast at 8. Therapies throughout the day until 6. Then dinner. Lights out by 9. Only the Sundays were different, with the children sitting in the chapel for Sunday Mass.

On this Sunday, Lucie had been excused from praise and was sitting alone in a large playroom, waiting. She looked around, not knowing why she had been asked to come here. No idea that it was for a visitor who had come to see her. She sat on one of the benches in front of the television, which was switched off.

With the nuns all at the service, a male orderly oversaw the running of the wing and didn't knock as he barged into the room, talking loudly.

"She's in here, okay?" he announced, shocking Lucie, making her wince in her seat.

Walking in behind the orderly, a woman in her fifties looked at Lucie, unable to hide her flicker of unease. She wore heavy makeup and clothes that mimicked luxury brands yet fell far short of real quality. Her poorly dyed hair completed the look of someone trying too hard without the money to pull it off believably.

As the orderly walked out, closing the door behind her, the woman was left standing awkwardly in the room without any introduction.

"Hello," she eventually said, stepping closer. "Do you know who I am, Lucie?"

Lucie, as always, remained silent.

The woman laughed nervously to herself. "Of course not. Of course you can't remember me. I mean, how could you? Last time I saw you, you were a baby. But my name. Odile. Aunt Odile. I'm your mother's sister."

An uncomfortable pause spread between them as her laughter dropped away.

"I... I didn't see her much, my sister, I mean," Odile continued. "When she had you, we were already not talking much." Wallowing for a second, she snapped herself out of it with a smile. "But I *do* remember you." She lifted her hands. "But I could hold you in my hands back then. You were so tiny."

Lucie's lack of reaction cut off her nostalgia, as Odile realized the falseness of this moment. She didn't know Lucie at all.

She moved closer and sat down beside her on the bench. Staring at the child's affectless look, Odile sighed.

"What the hell did they do to you?" she mumbled. "Who would do this?"

She put her hand comfortingly on Lucie's shoulder. A simple gesture that was met with Lucie immediately tensing.

Despite this reaction, Odile didn't move her hand and began to stroke the child's shoulder.

Letting out a panicked whimper, Lucie slid off her chair and ran to the other end of the room. Consumed with a sudden fear.

"Hey!" Odile complained, her feelings hurt, as she stood up.

Lucie, unblinking in horror, huddled against the corner of the room.

"Don't be afraid," Odile said, walking closer.

The bloodcurdling scream that Lucie let out was heard even in the chapel.

Odile sat in Doctor Coisson's office, a cigarette trembling in her hand. She took unsteady drags on it, clearly shaken by the experience.

"I assure you, Mrs. Manzor," the doctor explained. "Lucie is much better than she was. The time the police needed to complete their investigation was very beneficial to her recovery. Being here for so long with no other distractions has been key to her recovery."

"Yeah?" Odile answered, jitterily. "Sure doesn't seem like it. She acted like I was the one who kidnapped her."

"When she came in, she wasn't reactive at all. No crying, no words, no sounds, nothing that you would expect after someone who had gone through what she had."

Odile smirked, unamused. "Well, she reacts now, that's for damn sure."

"And that's a good thing... She also has a friend now, you know? Someone that she speaks to. That relationship has significantly contributed to her progress. However, you must understand that with adults, it's not so easy for her because adults did this to her. Over time, this will change."

Odile sighed. "I couldn't even tell her about her mother. Does she even know what happened to her?"

"We told her she had passed... As best we could,

anyway. I think she understood, but we cannot be too sure. She may not have believed us. Though she has not once asked for her mother, we think she is aware. The effect of her experience has made her reactions unpredictable. She may scream at a touch on the shoulder, yet not be fazed by the death of a parent."

Taking a longer drag, Odile exhaled loudly. "She never got to see Lucie after all that. After all she went through. She died before she could know that her daughter survived."

"It's most likely because she thought she'd never see Lucie again that she died so quickly."

Odile looked appalled at this. "Doctor, my sister did *not* kill herself."

"No, you misunderstood me, Mrs. Manzor. I simply mean grief hastened things. It's quite common that people with cancer, when suffering grief... just give in. They stop fighting. Especially when they live on their own. And with Lucie's mother in particular, her cancer spread with lightning speed, so the medical report said."

As she stubbed her cigarette out in the ashtray, Odile was at a loss. "I had no idea," she said. "I was just told she died of a tumor in her brain."

The doctor nodded. "And now, you are Lucie's only remaining family."

But Odile was not listening and was caught up in thoughts of her sister, getting more emotional. "Maybe if I came to visit her after Lucie went missing... I heard about it from a friend. But I didn't even call her. I didn't even try."

"I understand, but Lucie—"

"I don't even know Lucie," Odile snapped. "I met her once when she was born... That's it. Marthe and I stopped talking just after. And I don't even remember why. I don't know what made us—" she stopped herself talking as she fought to regain her composure.

"I'm not here to make you feel guilty, Mrs. Manzor. You have no legal obligations to Lucie. And you have until the judge signs a release order to consider it."

"I don't think I can do this," Odile said, mainly to herself.

The large office window was open, leading to the rose garden out back, letting in the cool air.

Outside, crouched under its sill, was Anna. Listening intently to all that was being said inside.

Visibly happy with what she had heard Odile say, Anna slipped out from her hiding place and crept back to the path, around the side of the building.

"What are you doing here?" the mother superior demanded as Anna came walking around the corner. "You should be in the park. The rose garden is out of bounds."

With an innocent smile, Anna acted perfectly. "Oh no, I'm so sorry. I got lost. This place is so big."

The mother superior was wise enough to know when a child was lying, even lying as believably as Anna could.

"Lost, huh?" she said. "Well, hurry up to the park. Dinner will be served soon."

As Anna ran off down the path, the mother superior could not help but chuckle.

On the east side of the rehabilitation center sat a large, walled-in park with a playground and a field, lined by a thicket of blossoming oak trees.

Some of the more active students played football on the field, while others sat on the grass, reading or simply enjoying the warmth of the day.

Indifferent to everyone else there, Anna skirted the pitch and headed straight to the oak trees. Their canopies cast a thick shadow onto the wild bushes below. Through these thorns and vines, a small path had been made that only two patients knew of.

With a smile on her face, Anna walked down the path to the trunk of one of the centuries-old trees. There, sat leaning against its trunk, was Lucie. Watching the other children at play through the branches.

As Anna sat down beside her, Lucie turned her gaze. The sounds of the joyful games from the other patients drifting over them.

"We *are* gonna stay together," Anna smiled. "She isn't going to take you away."

Slowly, Lucie smiled. An emotional and very genuine smile. Something that only Anna had ever seen.

They sat together in silence for a moment until Lucie went to stand up. With legs still weak and not yet fully healed, she staggered under her weight.

"Careful," Anna said, reaching her hand up— something Lucie accepted with ease.

Concentrating, she used Anna's grip to counterbalance.

"That's good," Anna said.

Proud that she managed it, Lucie let go of Anna's hand.

"You're getting much better at that," Anna said, but before Lucie could show any appreciation, the bushes broke open. A football from the field shot in at speed and slammed into Lucie. Sending her sprawling back into the thorny bushes.

As she screamed, a small boy quickly appeared, unaware of what had happened. Unaware that anyone else was even here.

"Idiot!" Anna shouted at the boy as she ran over to the now inconsolable Lucie. The thorns cut through her clothes and into her skin. Too weak to stand on her own again, she was only able to thrash about in agony.

The boy, Bertrand, was harmless. With Down's Syndrome, he looked worried at Lucie and nervously smiled. He tried to mumble an apology, but Anna's immediate rage eclipsed it.

"You stupid fuck!" she shouted. "Get out!"

Bertrand, instantly scared, turned and ran, not caring about the ball anymore. Just terrified of Anna.

As Lucie cried out, the thorns punctured her back

and arms. Anna quickly grabbed her. Not caring about the thorns that cut into her arms, too.

When Anna yanked Lucie to her feet, the thorns were dragged with her, caught in the knit of her woolen pullover. Lucie screamed again as they cut against her more, launching herself at Anna, wrapping her arms around her, and clinging on as tightly as she could.

"It's okay, shhhh," Anna said. "It's okay."

They did not walk back via the path, but instead stuck to the treeline, out of sight, until they reached the main building. Sneaking into one of the dark storerooms, Anna locked the door and helped Lucie to the floor, who was still sobbing in pain.

"You shouldn't cry," Anna said, crouching down in front of her. "All it does is hurt you more." Licking her thumb, she began wiping the blood away from the scratches on Lucie's hand. "Just tell yourself that pain is only a feeling. Something you don't have to care about. If you tell yourself that pain doesn't really hurt, it won't."

Lucie nodded sheepishly, wincing as Anna wiped a small smear of blood from her finger.

"It won't," Anna repeated. "Tell yourself that."

Anna looked unsure.

"Go on," Anna urged. "Do it now."

"It... doesn't... hurt," Lucie whispered in a small, unsure voice.

"It *doesn't* hurt," Anna echoed as she reached up

and pulled a small thorny twig stuck on Lucie's pullover. "Here, look."

Without a pause, Anna took the twig and pushed one of the thorns into the palm of her own hand. Not even twitching or showing any effect. Instantly, a thick drop of blood beaded up out of the punctured skin.

Staring at her new wound for a second, Anna then took Lucie's hand and looked for a bleeding scratch. Finding one on her wrist, she pressed her own wound against it. Mixing their red essences into one.

"We'll always be together," Anna smiled.

"What in the world is going on?" a nun standing behind them said. Neither girl had heard the door open. "What are you doing in here?"

Startled, Lucie and Anna looked back guiltily as if they had been caught in a crime.

Lucie pulled her hands away from Anna and cowered, pushing herself back against the shadowy wall and hiding her scratches.

"What the—" the nun started, seeing a quick flash of red on Anna's finger. "Show me your hands."

Reluctantly, Anna brought her hands up, catching the light coming in through the door and illuminating the thorn scratches and blood on her palm.

"Dear Lord, what did you do to yourself?" the nun said in shock.

Anna didn't answer, as Lucie remained scared, hiding her wounds as if punishment would follow if discovered.

"And you?" the nun turned to her. "Did you hurt yourself, too?"

"No, she didn't," Anna answered. "Just me. I fell into a bush outside."

"This and poor Bertrand having a seizure?" Shaking her head, the nun took Anna by the arm. "Come on, I'll disinfect this for you."

Lucie instinctively reached forward and clung to Anna's other arm, not wanting her to go.

Seeing this reaction, the nun sighed. "Lucie, please, let go. You'll see her after."

But Lucie remained, grabbing tight onto her friend.

"*Enough!*" the nun moaned, losing her temper. Scaring Lucie into letting go and retreating to the wall.

In the small infirmary, Anna sat on a stool as the nun dabbed iodine on the small wound on the palm of her hand.

On the small bed opposite was Bertrand. Having been found in convulsions after she scared him off, he was now asleep.

She looked at the boy, feeling a sense of guilt, wondering if her shouting at him had caused this.

"Anna, you're such a good girl," the nurse said, turning to get a band-aid. "You shouldn't start acting like her, do you understand me? She is not well."

Anna didn't answer.

"She's still very sick. You know, that don't you?"

The nurse continued as she stuck the band-aid onto her cleaned wound. "Don't you?" she repeated.

Anna nodded hesitantly.

The nurse spoke, carefully choosing her words. "She doesn't mean to, but she hurts herself a lot. And it's not an accident like falling onto some thorns... She needs rest. Lots of rest. And not someone leading her astray."

"Lucie!" came another nun's voice from the corridor.

Before Anna could turn, the door to the infirmary flew open and Lucie burst in. The other nun was trying to catch up to her.

"Come back here!" she called out again.

But Lucie wasn't listening. She ran straight into the room and wrapped her arms around Anna, looking absolutely petrified.

"You promise we'll always be together?" she whimpered.

The nuns shared a glance, not having heard Lucie speak before.

Anna held her as tightly back.

"And we will," she said. "Always."

Bertrand had woken, bleary-eyed from the noise, and now stared at Anna, as scared as he had been before.

———

The rehabilitation center had two large dormitories, each with thirty beds, one for boys and one for girls.

At the far end of the girls' dorm, Lucie and Anna were side by side in a single bed, trying to sleep. Lucie's bed lay untouched next to them. Having not slept in for a single night since they moved here.

Everyone was asleep. The room was quiet and dark. There were no plug-in night lights needed, as the window above let in a silver cascade of moonbeams.

Through the calm, a distant cry sounded from the next corridor. A quick, muffled sound made Lucie's body tense, as her eyes snapped open. She didn't realize it, but her breathing had become immediately stilted and loud.

"It's nothing, Lucie," Anna whispered, waking up from Lucie's gasps, putting a comforting arm around her. "Just someone having a nightmare in the boy's dorm."

Lucie didn't listen, though, as she stared at the double doors where the sound came in from.

"Just go back to sleep," Anna said.

"No," came Lucie's barely audible whisper. "They... They're coming."

Rubbing her eyes, Anna had to stifle her yawn. "They? Who?"

Lucie kept staring, too afraid to blink as she expected the door to open at any second.

"*Them...*"

. . .

The hospital corridor was lit only by neon fluorescence, with no windows to let in any light from outside, and at the far end sat a desk. Under the white glare, the orderly was there, dozing with his headphones on, the sound of his music keeping him from hearing the dormitory door creak open.

He was snoring to himself by the time Lucie had slipped out, barefoot in her hospital nightgown.

The corridor around her was silent, save for the buzzing of the strip lights, and she walked in the opposite direction. Not wondering which way to go, but creeping along as if drawn that way.

She was going back to the storeroom.

Step by cold step, she moved slowly, her eyes darting around to make sure no one was following.

Getting to the door, she stopped and took a breath before pushing it open.

This dark room was filled with brooms, mops, sheets, and bottles of cleaning chemicals. It looked the same as earlier, and still stank of bleach.

She let the door swing shut behind her.

The only light in here was coming in from a high-up window, casting a pale glare across her face.

She looked around and listened. There was no sound, yet she still felt a shiver.

"Who's there?" she asked.

Behind her was a stretch of metal shelving. She turned to look at the boxes upon them. But before she could take a step closer, she noticed a thick, almost oily shadow beside this shelf. A shadow that looked as though it had mass.

She stopped in her tracks and swallowed nervously.

"It's you, isn't it?"

The shadow then moved.

From within this darkness, an undulation of flesh shifted as a huge, naked creature lumbered toward her. It was soaked in so much blood that it dripped in heavy splats upon the storeroom floor. Open sores covered its filthy skin, with long, dark, matted hair clinging wetly to its shoulders. Its mouth couldn't open; its lips crudely stitched shut with thick twine.

It was female, but closer to a nightmare than a human.

"No!" Lucie screamed, collapsing to the floor. "I'm sorry!"

But the figure advanced on her, crooked as it limped. The sounds of its bones clacking against each other, as loud as the building moan of torment coming from its bound lips.

Lucie crawled back until her back hit another shelf, knocking an empty jar to the floor, which smashed into shards around her. The thing lunged, its broken fingernails slashing at the air at her face.

In her bed, Anna woke with a start, expecting to see Lucie beside her, but there was no one there. She didn't know why she had woken, as the room lay very silent, and the rest of the children were still soundly asleep.

Getting out of bed, she crept over to the door and pushed it open.

The orderly was snoring loudly, still wearing his headphones. He didn't hear the screams that drifted from the far end of the hall. The screams that made Anna panic as she ran toward them.

The storeroom door was flung open as Anna ran in.

Lucie was hunched on the floor, hysterical, with a shard of broken jar gripped in her hand. She carved it across her forearm, cutting a deep slice into her skin. Blood seeped down, pooling on the floor around her.

Her eyes were fixed on the space in front of her, where she saw the naked, grotesque creature clawing for her with broken, blood-soaked fingernails.

"Lucie, no!" Anna cried as she grabbed the glass shard from Lucie.

As it was taken, Lucie's perception suddenly shifted. The monstrous creature slashing at her was gone in an instant. Vanished. And in its place, Anna was crying at her.

"It's me! *It's me*! Please stop!"

"She's here," Lucie gasped, shaking her head, as her eyes darted around the darkness, trying to find out where her attacker had disappeared to. Her hands swatting at the air in front of her.

"There's no one here." Anna grabbed Lucie's arm

where the blood was dripping the thickest, and tightly pressed her palm against it.

Lucie began to settle as she looked down and noticed the self-inflicted wound. "No," she began to sob. "She hurt me, didn't she?" Collapsing into Anna's arms, Lucie cried out. "I'm sorry. I'm so sorry.".

Rocking her friend like a baby, Anna was crying too. "It's over. I'm here."

After a moment, she lifted Lucie's chin to look at her. "We have to go, okay? We should get some bandages. and—"

"Don't tell anyone," Lucie begged. "Please."

———

Two days went by, and Anna had not told a soul. She had taken Lucie to the infirmary that night, cleaned and wrapped her wounds, then had taken her back to the dormitory without a word.

Anna wanted to ask her what she saw, wanted to know who *they* were, but couldn't bring herself to upset her friend anymore.

CHAPTER THREE

FOLLOWED

"Everything's ready," the doctor smiled as he signed a form on his desk, then closed its manila folder. "The judge approved the custody papers after your petition, and the police have cleared it all from their end. Sorry it took so long, but with this kind of crime..."

Odile sat in the chair opposite, less in shock than the last time she was here. But she was still very worried, even though she had convinced herself that she *had* to do the right thing. The *charitable* thing. The *Christian* thing.

"Does she... remember any of what happened?" she asked, taking the folder from the doctor.

"That is the problem, Mrs. Manzor," he replied, detached from any emotion as usual. "Lucie remembers absolutely everything." He clicked his pen and placed it into his coat pocket. "Because of that, you shouldn't leave her alone for long periods of time just yet. And with her night terrors, you may wish to share a room with her, at least for the first few nights."

Odile dreaded this, but steeled herself. "What do I do with night terrors?" she asked. "I've never had a child. Especially not one like..." her words trailed off.

"Quite simple. You wake her. Talk to her. Tell her it's over. Remind her it's just a nightmare. That she is safe."

———

As the morning sun shone through the high windows in the dormitory, the children were awake and dressing. The 8 a.m. bell had sounded, and breakfast was soon ready to be served.

But as they all filed out, Anna was left looking about. She had noticed that the locker at the end of Lucie's bed had been opened and emptied. Her few clothes and possessions were taken.

Worried, she stepped out of the dormitory and immediately saw the orderly ahead of her, carrying a cardboard box and leading the way to the exit. The mother superior followed closely behind, with Lucie trailing after them, her head lowered, dressed not in a hospital gown but in regular clothes, complete with a large winter jacket.

"Lucie!" Anna called, running after them.

Lucie stopped and turned, looking forlorn and exhausted.

"What's happening? Where are you going?" Anna asked, quickly catching up.

But the mother superior stepped between them.

"Go back to breakfast, Anna," she said sternly.

"But—" Anna's voice broke.

"Lucie's going to her home now." She said with a smile.

As she did, Lucie seemed to deflate more.

"She *can't* go," Anna said desperately, meeting Lucie's sad gaze. "We made that promise, remember. We said we'd stay together."

Lucie smiled as best as she could.

"Always, Anna," she said. "Always." The words seemed to hurt her to speak.

As the mother superior turned and guided Lucie away. Anna was left standing in the corridor in shock, watching as her only friend was taken away.

Standing outside the hospital entrance, Lucie looked up at her aunt, who was beside her, busily lighting her cigarette.

"Well, I guess, it's just the two of us now," Odile said, forcing a smile. "Come on. Let's go home."

As she walked out onto the gravel driveway, she quickly noticed that Lucie was not following. She remained in place by the door, looking nervous.

"You'll see, it'll be fine," Odile said, stepping back and taking Lucie's hand. "We'll have a great adventure, and you'll be safe, okay?"

As the orderly put the box of Lucie's belongings in the back of Odile's car, he slammed the trunk shut, the noise making Lucie jolt.

Odile already sensed how hard this was going to be. "It's fine... Please... Now come along."

After tugging lightly on her hand, Lucie reluctantly took a step forward

Behind her, she did not see Anna at the window of the dormitory, looking down, crying.

———

That night, the dormitory was colder and quieter than usual for Anna. She did not hear the breaths of her friend next to her, nor feel the heat from her skin.

Now, her small bed felt immense and lonely.

Then came a noise.

Something from deep inside the building. Like the sound Lucie described hearing so many times before. A small sound, barely perceptible, was now audible for the first time, and Anna stared toward the door, frightened.

On the other side of Paris, in Pont-de-Flandre in the 19th arrondissement, a small house stood on a quiet street.

The attic had been converted into a small bedroom. Newly painted with a crucifix on the wall above the small bed, it was warm and cozy, a far cry from the winter night outside.

But still, Lucie was under the covers, shivering. Scared. Listening to the sounds around the room. A faint scratching sound that came from inside the walls. It started as a slight, infrequent murmur, but quickly became a louder and more intense sound on the plaster.

Scrape.

Scrape.

Lucie pulled the bedsheets up to her chin.

Scrape.

Scrape.

Outside the small window, the trees cast their shadows onto the white curtains. Appearing in Lucie's mind like arms reaching to get inside.

She squeezed her eyes shut as hard as she could, silently wishing the noises and shadows away.

But they stayed.

Scrape.

Scrape.

It then got even louder.

"Please," she whispered through gritted teeth, refusing to look.

Scrape.

Scrape.

"*Please,*" she pleaded again, even harder, as her breath started to quicken. "*Please. Please. Please. I'll do anything.*"

Then, as if by command, the noises stopped on that

last word. Leaving in their place a silence that immediately consumed the room with a pressure. A pressure that forced Lucie to open her eyes again, as she held her breath.

There was only darkness. The shadows on the other side of the curtains were just harmless branches once more, swaying gently in the moonlight.

She allowed herself to exhale, that is, until the gnarled hand reached out from the darkness and grabbed her by the ankle.

Odile woke with the sound of Lucie's screams.

Since getting back to her house, the evening had been a morose one. With Lucie not saying a word, she had walked through her new home like a ghost. She had eaten dinner, sat watching television, all without paying much attention to anything. Then she went to bed before the clock had hit 8 p.m.

Now, at twelve past midnight, from the room above Odile's bed, she was screaming.

"Lucie," she called, hastily tying her dressing gown up as she took two steps at a time up to the attic room.

When she got to the top of the narrow staircase, Odile opened the door to see Lucie in a corner, next to the small nightlight, in floods of tears. Her arms wrapped around her face to protect her from whatever had come at her in her mind.

"Lucie, what is it?" Odile asked, switching on the light and looking around the small room. There was nothing there. Bed. Drawers. Chair. The window was shut. The cupboard was closed.

With a trembling hand, Lucie slowly pointed to the bed, her eyes locked on her aunt.

For a moment, Odile worried that there may be something in here. But as she bent down to check under the bed, she quickly realized that this was precisely what the doctor had warned her about.

"There's nobody there, do you see?" she asked, lifting the skirt of the bed, showing the large space underneath.

Lucie shook her head, not wanting to look.

"She *was* there," she said.

These were the first words that Odile had heard Lucie speak.

In surprise, she lowered the skirt and crouched down beside her.

"Who was there?" she asked.

Lucie slowly dared to open her eyes, to look under the bed. "The woman."

"It was a nightmare," Odile spoke calmly and comfortingly. "You're so safe now. The house is locked up. No one is here except you and me. And I am here to protect you."

"She is..." Lucie said, squeezing her eyes shut again. "She's here." She pressed herself against the wall as hard as she could. "She's *so angry*."

Odile's voice softened more. "It's over, sweetheart. I'm here. I'm here."

. . .

After putting Lucie back to her bed and trying her best to convince her that no one was in her room, Odile went back downstairs to try to sleep. It was 1:25 a.m. and she couldn't even remember the last time she'd been up this late... early... whichever it was. Maybe when she was a teenager, but not for many, many years.

As she was about to fall asleep again, Odile's mind kept waking her back up, expecting to hear more screaming upstairs. So there she lay, awake in the dark, staring at the ceiling.

She then heard a faint creak in the hallway outside the room, as the door started to open.

Suddenly worried that Lucie may be right, and there could possibly be someone in the house, Odile smiled in relief as she saw Lucie. There in the doorway, barefoot and scared.

"Lucie?" Odile asked. "Are you okay?"

She didn't answer, and only she bowed her head, feeling ashamed. "I'm sorry," she murmured.

"Don't be silly," Odile replied, sitting up. "Come here."

Lucie didn't move.

With a sigh, Odile switched on her lamp and got out of bed. "You scared me, Lucie. I told you it was just a dream. You know it was."

"But she's still here," came the nervous reply. "She's in the walls. I can hear her."

"No, my dear. There's no one." Odile chanced putting a comforting hand on the girl's arm. Lucie didn't back away or flinch from her touch. "You should sleep with me tonight," she said as she led Lucie to the bed. "Get in, it's okay. I'll protect you, I swear."

After the light was turned off, Odile had drifted back off to sleep with ease, thinking that would be the end of it for the night, when...

Scratch.

Scratch.

Scratch.

Lucie stared at the wall beside her, hearing the noises coming from the other side of the wallpapered plasterboard. A noise that got louder and louder.

Scratch.

Scratch.

Scratch.

Lucie reached back to grab her aunt. "She's here," she said.

Odile woke back up, blinking herself into attention, getting aggravated.

"What?"

Scratch.

Scratch.

Scratch.

The lamp was turned on again, as the noises were getting more frantic.

Scratch.

Scratch.

Scratch.

Odile couldn't hear a thing and shook her head.

"It's a dream, that's all," she said.

But in Lucie's ears, the sound was unrelenting and in full force.

Scratch.

Scratch.

Scratch.

Odile raised her hand and stroked Lucie's hair. "Shhhh, now. Go back to sleep."

Lucie couldn't hear those words over her own fear and sank into the sheets, pulling them over her face. Hiding.

Scratch.

Scratch.

Scratch.

Then it stopped, and as it did, the lamp beside the bed flickered.

Something Odile *did* see.

But she thought better of thinking that anything insidious could be happening, so she switched off the lamp. Desperate to get back to sleep.

The morning rose a few hours later, and Odile sat at the breakfast table, drinking her second cup of coffee in a row. She was tired and didn't even have the energy to eat her croissant. It sat on the plate in front of her.

Lucie was the same; she wasn't touching her breakfast.

"You've gotta eat something," Odile said, motioning to Lucie's plate. "You need your strength." She glanced down at her own breakfast and realized her double standards. Picking up the croissant, she took a bite to urge her niece on. To set an example.

Lucie didn't move.

"If you don't eat, you might have to go back to the center," she added, trying to be funny and failing.

Lucie's gaze flicked over to hers, giving Odile a sudden shock of concern.

"Wait, you don't *want* that, do you? To go back there?"

Lucie's reply was quiet. "It's better there," she said.

Taken aback, Odile paused. "But that place was full of people, and that wasn't safe, was it? All those people coming and going. Here you have a house. Locks on the door. Much better food. A nicer bed. And... you have family... You have me."

Lucie looked down, breaking eye contact. "But Anna..." was all she could say.

Odile forced a smile that she didn't feel at all. "It's okay, it's only been one night. You'll get used to it soon, and you will love this house as much as I do. We'll have so much fun, won't we? Think of all the adventures we will have."

Shaking her head slowly, Lucie closed her eyes, stopping herself from crying at the thought.

Odile's smile faltered as she lifted her cup, holding its handle tightly to stop losing her calm.

———

Later that week, a storm had broken over Paris, covering the city in a constant downpour and gale-force winds.

At 9 p.m., as the drains on the road started to overflow, Lucie was lying in bed, delaying sleep as she dreaded the nighttime. Dreaded hearing that awful scratching in the walls. Dreaded seeing that woman.

Lucie was drawing on a pad of paper. The thick felt pen crudely sketched a gaunt face, with dark, black holes for eyes. After she completed its jagged-toothed grimace, she stared at the drawing for a moment, then moved her hand and added four vertical lines down it, as if they were bars keeping the woman inside the drawing.

Bang.

The felt pen cut across the page as Lucie looked up.

The shutter had slammed against the window frame, blown loose of its latch, and now flapped wildly.

But it wasn't the window that then took her attention. It was her bedroom door. Her now open door, that she could have sworn had been closed.

As the rain hammered on the window, Lucie looked around, feeling very much in danger.

At the bottom of the attic staircase, Lucie appeared from the doorway, scared as she peered out. Her attention was pulled to the bathroom door. It had been left half open with the light on, but flickering.

"Aunty?" she quietly called out.

Hugging her arms, she silently crept along the hallway.

"Aunt Odile?" she said again.

As she drew closer to the bathroom, she could see the steam from the hot water filling the room, clouding the mirror.

"Hello?" she asked.

Inside, the freestanding, ornate bathtub was overflowing with hot water, the faucet still running, and soaking the floor tiles.

But there was no one in there.

Not knowing what else to do, Lucie reached out and turned the water off. Her feet stung as she stood in the hot water.

She turned and looked out into the hallway.

"Aunt Odile?" she called out louder. Getting as worried for her aunt as she was scared for herself.

With the sound of the running water ceased, the slight splash of something large moving in the tub behind her was enough for her to stop. Her eyes shot up to the mirror, and there in the fogged-up glass was a shape moving behind her.

Whirling, Lucie saw it. The thing that had not been there a second ago was now very much in existence.

The creature, with its back to her. Naked and monstrous. And in this light, for the first time, Lucie saw the damage over her with absolute clarity.

The skin on its back had been flayed off long ago.

The exposed flesh and bone were a putrid yellow, riddled with a severe infection. The open sores over the rest of its body were even more horrific. The thing's hair was long, thin, and patchy over her scabbed head.

The creature slowly turned, until its black, hollow eye sockets faced her, and it opened its mouth —its stitched mouth. The twine holding her lips together cut through her flesh as she forced her jaw open. Each stitch ripping loose, tearing her skin open. Dark blood spilled out of her mouth as she let out a horrifying moan. She exposed a painful row of brown, cracked teeth, with ends jagged from being smashed.

Lucie screamed as she went to run away, but the water beneath her feet made her slip on the wet tile. Her body spun as she caught herself on the edge of the sink. Narrowly avoiding falling over.

And the tub was empty again. The water within it, sloshing about, freshly disturbed.

Lucie's eyes darted around the bright room, her breathing getting shorter and shorter, not knowing which way or where she could run.

Odile woke up to the sound of screaming yet again.

Shaking her head, she grumbled her way to the bedroom door.

Looking into the hallway, Lucie darted past her, bawling.

"Lucie?"

But she ran down the stairs and straight to the front door.

Fumbling with the chain, Lucie's hands shook out of control as she tried to unlock it.

"Lucie, stop, please!" Odile called out, walking down the stairs after her. "It's just a dream."

But her words made no difference, as Lucie managed to free the chain, throw open the door, and disappear into the storm outside.

"*Lucie!*"

The rain outside was louder than her call, and even if it wasn't, Lucie wasn't stopping for anyone.

Sprinting barefoot down the middle of the street, she ran over the puddled asphalt as an oncoming car caught her in its headlights, slammed on its horn, and swerved to miss her.

Lucie wasn't thinking as she ran, eyes wild, screaming constantly into the battering storm.

She couldn't stop.

She darted between the beams of other cars, almost getting hit, until she ran onto the sidewalk and vanished into the night.

Odile's futile cries muffled in the distance.

The farther Lucie ran, the sharper the pain in her feet became. The rough ground below scraped her bare soles raw. Each step she took sent a wave of soreness up her legs. It felt like she was running on ice as the puddles splashed up around her ankles.

Her sodden nightdress clung to her small body, but still, she pushed herself forward, out of breath and screaming in panicked bursts.

Fear was the only thing keeping her going.

She had nothing else left.

Gradually, the city around her changed. Houses and shops dwindled, replaced by industrial buildings, empty lots, all heavy with shadows. With exhaustion catching up, Lucie stumbled, collapsing beside a chain-link fence that bordered a dark factory.

Sprawled on a patch of uneven, muddy grass, she stared around, gasping.

The storm above blossomed, as lightning started to tear across the sky in blinding flashes, with thunder crashing in its wake.

Lucie was devastated, beyond rational sense.

And with each burst of lightning that followed, she saw it.

Saw her.

That creature.

She had not escaped it.

It first appeared far down the road.

Then behind the opposite fence.

Then closer.

Never in the same place twice, and only for the instant the sky flashed.

But each time staring at Lucie. Her torn mouth open. Her arms reaching out, clawing at her.

Lucie could do nothing more. She could not run

anymore. All she could do was curl into herself, shivering in the rain, sobbing in helpless anguish.

————

The missing persons reports turned up very little.

Some reported a girl matching Lucie Jurin's description all across the city.

One person claimed to have seen her stealing from a trash can outside a petrol station on the A6.

A cab driver reported seeing someone matching her description walking along the verge in the rain; he said he slowed, offered to call someone, and even offered to take her home, but she ran away and disappeared down a nearby embankment.

A municipal worker noticed a small girl sleeping in a sewer tunnel, somewhere even the homeless junkies avoided.

However, all accounts were similar in that they were vague. And all were half-glimpsed moments that had little certainty.

Months had passed, and the sightings continued, but soon began to dwindle in frequency.

Odile Manzor had appeared on local television and radio, pleading for Lucie to come home, but as time went on, the description itself became useless. The photo in the newspaper became useless. The child who fled the house no longer resembled the one that people claimed to see.

What began as a short, thin eleven-year-old child

with a rough mop of brown hair became a taller young woman, with longer hair and a harsher face, carved through puberty.

———

Three years later, a caring priest reported '*a teenager, maybe fourteen*' begging for money outside his church in Marley Le Roi. When he asked her name, with ten francs offered as an incentive, the girl answered nervously. '*Lucie*' before hurriedly walking away.

The police followed up on every report filed, but every report came to nothing.

———

As the years blurred together, even Odile stopped her search, resigning herself to the idea that wherever Lucie was, she must be happier than she was with her.

Lucie's sixteenth birthday came and went with the same fanfare as any other day in February. Quietly and unceremoniously.

With her hair long and covering her face, she hid her gaze from any passing cars as she walked along the empty stretch of narrow road. With a battered backpack slung over her shoulder, she was a long way out of the city and had travelled far into the countryside. Large, empty fields spread out on both sides of the road and reached both horizons.

As a distant sound rumbled behind her, Lucie stopped without much thought and stepped off the road. Waiting for a moment, she did not react as a large delivery truck roared past, blasting its horn in thanks without slowing.

And as quickly as it approached, the vehicle was gone from sight, taking its noise along with it.

Glancing around, Lucie stepped back onto the road and carried on her walk into the silence.

This was a walk she had done before.

And for now, it would be the same. She would go searching.

She passed the road sign.

Chamfors 3km.

CHAPTER FOUR
HAPPY HOMES

1986

Lucie's twenty-sixth birthday came and went, and she looked nothing like she once had. Her hair was now cropped short, and she wore black jeans and a heavy army jacket. A long backpack hung from one shoulder and weighed her down. She was still slim, but taller, and her face had shed almost all its former innocence. Only her eyes remained unchanged since the day she first fled Aunt Odile's house. Restless, wary, watching everything with a nervous hawkishness.

And when she saw the cluster of rooftops appearing in the distance, basking in the midday sun, she couldn't hold in her smile.

These suburbs didn't look familiar, but she was confident that it was the right place.

At the far end of the serpentine roads that made up the housing estate, she had found it: Allée Jean

Baptiste Charlemagne. In all, a short row of houses that faced a wide stretch of woodland. Each home was modest, set behind a white picket fence and gate. Ordinary two-story homes, with beige walls, blue shutters, and long gravel-lined driveways.

She stopped at the house she had come to see—number six.

Putting down her backpack onto the ground in front of her, Lucie's breathing quickened. Reaching into her pocket, she brought out a small clipping from a local newspaper.

An article with a photo of a family smiling: Husband, wife, son, and daughter.

She glanced at it, then at the house.

Nodding to herself, she took a breath.

Today was the day.

———

Gabrielle Belfond was in her late forties and wore a large, white knitted jumper over a pair of jeans. Her hair was purposefully curled and dyed a chestnut red. Standing at the kitchen counter, she was busily making sandwiches for her family.

Antoine, her nineteen-year-old son, always had cheese and ham. Marie, her seventeen-year-old daughter, always had tuna. Paul, her husband, was happy with whatever was given. They were a family of tradition, no matter how small.

Walking in the front door, Paul Belfond was carrying a bag of groceries.

"The wanderer returns," he announced with a smile, entering the kitchen.

Antoine and Marie both returned his smile from their places at the table.

As Gabrielle spoke, she didn't take her eyes off making the sandwich.

"D'you get the mayo, hun?" she asked.

"Of course I did!"

"And the chocolate?" Marie asked excitedly.

"Yes, yes, what do you think I am? A failure of a father or something?" He leaned in and placed a kiss on his wife's cheek before putting the grocery bag on the counter, then started to unpack it.

First out of the bag, he pulled a bottle of wine, which didn't go in the fridge but was placed straight on the breakfast table.

"Anyone know where the corkscrew is?" he asked.

Gabrielle, plating up two of the sandwiches, picked them up and walked over to her children. "In the top drawer," she said. "Next to the towels, same place they've been for years."

"Well, I knew *that*," Paul laughed. "I was just testing you." Finishing the unpacking, he rummaged in the top drawer, picked up the corkscrew, and took it to the table.

He noticed the open toolbox on the floor by the counter, with a wrench and a hammer sticking out of the top.

"What broke?" he asked.

"Mom fixed the water pressure," Marie said, taking a bite of her sandwich.

Paul sat down. "Oh yeah?"

"Guess what was blocking it?" Gabrielle asked with a smile.

"Dunno. Hair?"

Marie laughed. "A mouse!"

Paul looked at his wife with pride. "What would I do without you, my dear?"

"Be overrun with vermin," she shrugged.

With everyone at the table and a fresh sandwich in front of each, the Belfond family began to eat. They talked with big smiles and a loving ease.

"Oh, Dad," Antoine said, sounding excited. "You wanna go see the racing later?"

Paul smirked. "Don't you mean, 'Oh Dad, can you give me a lift to and from the racing as I still haven't got my driving license, and I can't ride my bike there'"

"That's exactly what I said," Antoine laughed in reply.

"Well, as you are so kind to invite me, of course I would."

Gabrielle looked at her daughter. "And what are you planning to do today?"

Marie shrugged. "Dunno, was thinking about going to the cinema, maybe? Jacqui and Bea are going, but I haven't decided yet."

"Awesome food as always, my dear," Paul said with a mouthful.

She smiled. "Oh, did Antoine tell you his big plans?"

Paul nodded. "He did indeed. I was wondering what you thought about it."

"What I thought?" she asked. "What do you think I thought?"

Marie leaned over and patted her brother on the shoulder. "Hey, big brother, you want to quit a fifty-thousand-a-year school after three months?" she said. "That's one hell of a ballsy move."

"It is indeed," Gabrielle nodded. "Especially as we paid a whole year in advance."

Antoine just stared at his sandwich, trying to avoid any of the conversation.

Marie laughed, "So, come on, Ant. Tell us why?"

The boy sighed. "Law just doesn't feel right, okay?"

"But law leads to everything," Paul smiled.

Ding Dong.

The doorbell rang and everyone turned toward it.

"Expecting anyone?" Gabrielle asked Paul, who shook his head in response.

"Maybe Luc?" he said, standing up. "He said he may come over to borrow the mower."

As he left the room, Gabrielle looked at her son.

"Three months," she said incredulously. "We'll talk about it later. Now finish your food."

Gabrielle looked at her family, and even with any disagreements or trouble, she thought their life was idyllic. That they were perfect despite their imperfections, everything in their life was just how she always imagined and hoped it would be.

Opening the front door, Paul looked out, expecting to see one of his neighbors.

Instead, he saw the barrel.

Boom.

His chest blew apart as he flew back down the hallway.

"Paul?" she shouted as she stood up.

"What was that noise?" Marie gasped.

"Dad?" Antoine called out, worried.

From the kitchen, Gabrielle walked out. As she did, her smile dropped, and she ran back inside.

"Get—" she didn't get to warn her children.

Boom.

The shot collided with her back. Sending her across the table, smashing into the food as glass and blood sprayed everywhere. The whiteness of this spread was soon drenched in her gloopy redness.

Antoine didn't have much time to react, staring in abject horror at his mother's body, now splayed out in front of him.

Boom.

Another shot, close enough to him that it demolished the entire left side of his head. Opening it up, with brain, bone, and gore falling out beside him, as well as drenching his sister.

Marie screamed as the gun was reloaded with a detached calm.

"Mom, Dad," She cried as she dropped down behind the kitchen table, sobbing.

"Please, please, don't," she begged, her eyes squeezed shut to try and trap out the horrors that just befell his family.

Click.

The gun stalled.

Lucie stood there, opening the weapon's breech. She checked the cartridge, taking it out and quickly replacing it. She did so with a cold shrug.

Walking around the table, she saw Marie, looking up terrified, her hands held up defensively.

"Please," was all she said.

For a second, as Lucie looked down at the girl's innocent and distraught face, she hesitated. But only for that second.

After she pulled the trigger, the sobbing stopped, and Lucie was left with a smoking shotgun in the middle of the bloody massacre she had wrought.

The only sound now was the sound of the clock on the wall, ticking away the seconds of the day.

She lowered the shotgun and looked around the room, beyond the dead bodies. There were photographs and family trophies on the shelves. All spattered in blood.

Lucie didn't see the horror of the situation. Just the relief she felt.

"I did it," she whispered with a smile. "I really did it."

Walking back toward the front door, she opened it and sat down on the porch, exhausted. With the shotgun resting between her knees, she looked out into the yard. She felt a huge weight now lifted from her whole being. And for the first time since she could remember, she felt a serenity drifting over her. A deep calm that felt as foreign, but beautiful.

Feeling a wetness on her head, Lucie looked up to the sky. Small, cold droplets from the sky landed softly on her face. She couldn't hold back a laugh. A relieved and happy laugh that had eluded her for most of her life.

Finally.

Finally.

Finally.

From behind her, a noise broke her smile. A faint groan from the kitchen.

Lucie turned sharply, the smile gone, and the shotgun gripped in her hands once more.

The kitchen was quiet, as water from a shattered pitcher on the sideboard dripped onto the tiled floor below.

Lucie cautiously walked in, taking a moment to look around at the bodies. A sudden nervousness in her gaze as she half-expected the dead to return to life to come after her.

Her breathing started to quicken as she looked at her victims, one by one.

It *was* only then that she realized that one of the bodies had gone.

Gabrielle was no longer sprawled on the table.

From the far side of the kitchen, the groan sounded again.

Lucie stepped around the table, the shattered glass on the floor cracking under her weight. She followed the trail of blood that had smeared across the floor, leading out through the door to the utility room.

Carefully walking nearer, Lucie held the gun out, ready, and pushed open the door with her elbow.

There on the floor, Gabrielle was still alive, despite the large wound on her back, bleeding heavily yet still conscious. She tried to crawl to the back door with the bit of strength she had left.

Hearing glass crack behind her, Gabrielle weakly turned her head to see Lucie.

"Why," she gurgled.

But Lucie felt no pity for her, nor for anyone she killed. She trembled, but only through adrenaline, and aimed the gun.

"Do you remember me?" she said, stepping forward.

But Gabrielle looked back at her, confused and scared, and shook her head.

"*Liar!*" Lucie shouted as she kicked the woman in

the side. *"Liar! Liar! Liar!"* Each word came with another powerful kick.

Gabrielle tried her best to turn and crawl to the door, painfully as she tried.

"You don't get to run away! You don't get to escape! You NEVER get to escape!"

She pulled the trigger.

Gabrielle got the full force of the shot to her neck.

Panting, Lucie lowered the gun, cocked the barrels, and reloaded from two cartridges in her pocket.

She began to roar with rage as she lifted the gun again. "There's no fucking escape!" she shouted as she pulled the trigger again. "No fucking escape!" Her yells became cries as she fired the final shot into the back of Gabrielle's head.

In a daze, Lucie made her way back to the living room, the shotgun dragging behind her as she collapsed into an armchair, allowing the smile to return to her face.

"It's over now," she whispered to herself. "It's over."

Anna Assaoui, twenty-five, was still in bed, having only just woken up after a long shift at the hospital. With her uniform in a pile by the door of her studio apartment, she was dreading having to go back there today. She didn't want another day of dealing with blood and bodily fluids. She didn't want another day of being bossed around. It was a menial job that she had no choice but to do.

The phone's ringing was so loud that it made her sit bolt upright.

Taking a second, she shook her head to focus before reaching for the receiver.

"Hello?" she said, forcibly sounding as if she had been up for hours.

"*It's me.*"

"Lucie?" Anna replied instantly. "Where are you? I tried to call."

Lucie looked out the doorway and into the bloody kitchen as she grasped the phone with both hands.

"Chamfors," she said, almost in a dreamlike state. "I saw them. I *had* to see... They changed... but it was definitely them."

"*You went without me?*"

No response.

"*How can you be so sure?*"

Lucie smiled. "I'm telling you, it's them."

After a beat of stunned silence, Anna got out of bed, still holding onto the phone. "Lucie, it's been fifteen years... you were only a kid. You can't be expected to remember each—"

"*It's them!*" Lucie cut in with a flash of annoyance.

"Okay, okay, so you found that picture in the paper, and now you've confirmed it?"

Lucie didn't reply.

"So we'll do what we said we'd do. We'll call the cops. Get them arrested. Get justice."

"No. There's no point."

"What? What do you mean? That's the whole reason you're doing this."

"I already did what had to be done."

Anna paused. Her blood ran cold. An immediate dread crept over her as she realized that something bad had happened. "Lucie... *What* had to be done?"

"They won't hurt anyone else."

Anna was quickly approaching the verge of panic. "This wasn't the plan! I was supposed to be there with you. We were gonna go this weekend and observe them. You weren't sure. Remember you telling me that? You didn't really know. So we were *both* going to find out. Together."

"Why don't you believe me?"

Anna closed her eyes.

"I do... I do believe you... Now, where are you? Back home?"

"I'm in their house."

"Their house?"

At the other end of the line, Lucie sounded so proud and happy.

"I feel happy now."

Anna swallowed, and it felt like a knife in her

throat. She looked around and, with her spare hand, grabbed a pair of jeans from the closet.

"I'm coming. You stay right there, okay?" she pleaded.

"Okay, but hurry," Lucie said, before giving the address and hanging up the phone.

She felt giddy. Elated. She had finally found these after fifteen years of searching. After so long of combing the streets of Chamfors, Mirepoix, and all the surrounding areas. It was only when she chanced upon a local newspaper that she saw the photo.

The people in it looked older, but Lucie was sure that it was them. Paul, Gabrielle, Antoine, and Marie Belfond. The were the names under the picture, and it took Lucie a while to find out where they lived, but now that she was here, she could feel it was all worth it. Worth the years of searching. Worth the fear of confrontation. Now, she felt like she had won the war not just for herself but for others like her.

Anna's Renault sped past the stormy city limits, an open street map on the passenger seat. The windscreen wipers thudded back and forth as they washed the raindrops away.

With a small thermos of coffee in one hand, she had her foot on the pedal as far as it would go—though her car was old and hardly able to get above sixty miles an hour. It chugged along as fast as it could.

The shotgun lay on Lucie's lap as she sat motionless on the armchair again, staring through the doorway where she could see Antoine Belfond draped over his chair at the kitchen table. His head slung back and to the side, and his open skull now empty. Its contents splattered on the floor below him. His one remaining eye glaring straight at her.

But his glare just made her happy. And now, she was just like a little girl, her expression indifferent to the presence of the lives she had stolen.

A sudden creak from another room snapped her out of her stupor.

The childlike look vanished, replaced with worry as she listened, alert.

A second creak.

Getting to her feet, she turned to the front door. It creaked a third time as the storm outside started to build. She could see the empty porch and realized that nothing was causing the creaking sound apart from natural elements.

Opening the barrel of her gun, she tossed out the empty cartridges and went into her pocket to find more, but there was only one left.

The front door, meanwhile, continued to creak as it swayed in the wind.

She placed the cartridge in the barrel and snapped it shut.

The curtains in the living room rippled as the wind blew in harder.

Then.... *BANG.*

The wind swirled around the house and slammed the front door shut, making Lucie jump in a panic and pull on the trigger by mistake.

The shotgun blasted, and the skirting board in front of her exploded into shards of splintered wood.

Despite knowing there was nothing there, it didn't make her any less anxious.

Then another creak. Not from the front door this time. But in front of her.

"Mother fucker!" she gasped, dropping the empty gun to the carpet as her hands clambered through her pockets, searching for another weapon. Averting her eyes from the living room, so she could not see what was there.

She quickly pulled out her wood-handled straight razor.

As the rain pelted onto the windows, the house around her started to feel like a growing vacuum. A pressure began to build in her ears that she couldn't shake. A pressure she always felt when—

She rushed back into the kitchen, straight over to Antoine's slumped body, and put her hand inside the open wound in his skull. Drenching her fingers in the redness inside.

Pulling it back out, she, too preoccupied in her

mind to feel the grotesquerie of what she had done, walked back into the living room, averting her eyes from where the creak sounded, and raised her bloody hand, palm up, in its direction.

The pressure in her head was getting worse and worse, so much that she winced from its forceful ache. A small gasp escaped her lips as she squeezed her eyes shut.

"I did it," she said, as she started to lose control. The whole event was catching up to her.

The creak came again in front of her. She lowered her head and gritted her teeth.

"Leave me alone... please. What more can I do for you? I'm sorry!"

She then dared to open her eyes and look.

What was there was not the female creature, but one of the others. The many others who had followed her from her broken psyche.

At the other side of the living room, in a dark corner, behind the sofa, the body of a small boy was on the floor. With skin cracked and red, hair in patches, his body spasmed. And each spasm creaked on the uneven floorboard.

The boy's head cricked from side to side as the spasms made his body contort, until suddenly his back arched upward and he raised himself on his hands and feet like a human spider. From its toothless maw a sinister growl came, and he suddenly crawled around the sofa like a cockroach.

Lucie screamed as she backed away, swiping the razor in front of her.

The boy scuttled across the room, its weight thumping the floor as it went, as it then impossibly crawled up the wall, over the top of the doorway, and disappeared further into the house.

Filled with fear and anguish, Lucie still held up her bloodied hand.

"I did it," she yelled. "You shouldn't be here."

She was not presenting her hand to the boy, but to the other thing that was nearby. The thing she felt. The thing that was breathing loudly in her mind. The thing that then let out a small moan.

"See?" Lucie held her bloody hand out as far as she could, getting overcome with emotion. "It's over! You can leave now! Leave me alone!... Please... leave me alone."

The groans then stopped.

But it did not make Lucie any calmer. It made her worse.

Her breathing began to stutter as she looked around the room.

"*Why are you still here?!*" she cried out, then suddenly realized something. That she had not searched the rest of the house, that someone else could be here. Upstairs. That some*thing* was here because it was unfinished.

Frantically gripping the straight razor, she ran out of the room, into the hallway. Stopping for a moment at the base of the stairs to listen intently for any noise coming down.

But there was nothing.

Climbing up, her eyes darted around her, up and down, on the ceilings and walls. Looking for any possible or impossible thing lying in wait.

Reaching the top, she slowly approached the first closed door and opened it.

It was Marie's bedroom, and she looked around at the pink walls, pink bedsheets, and the Duran Duran posters. The dolls she had kept from her childhood. But no one was in there. It didn't matter, though, as Lucie walked in, razor held high as she pulled the sheets off the bed, opened the cupboards, and opened the drawers. Books, clothes, and possessions went flying as she ransacked the room. She *had* to check every single corner. Every single space. She needed to make sure it was done.

Lucie could not see the humanity in this room; she could only see what she knew in her mind.

"Devils," she grimaced.

Next was Antoine's room. There, she felt the same amount of justifiable hatred. But like Marie's room, here was also empty. She began tearing that one apart, too. Each drawer was removed and upturned. Every shelf emptied.

When done, she moved back into the hallway; only three doors remained. The stairs to the attic. The bathroom. The master bedroom.

The bathroom was empty and had nothing to overturn.

The attic would be last; she would check the bedroom first.

Her hand moved to the doorknob, but before she could turn it, a faint sound came from inside.

A scratch. A familiar scratch. *THAT* scratch.

Lucie yanked her hand back as she realized what it was, and could only guess what it meant.

That *thing* was in there. Maybe it was showing her where another person was hiding.

She pushed the door open, holding the razor up, ready to cut.

With a large four-poster bed and surrounded by floral wallpaper, it was like the rest of the house, homely, sweet, and picture-perfect.

The sunlight filtered through the curtains, shining on the far wall.

Lucie's pulse throbbed in her ear, but was soon eclipsed by another sickening sound. A guttural breathing now coming from behind her.

As she turned, she was met by the face of the thing. The creature. Same as it always was. Putrid, monstrous, and with most of its rancid skin flayed off. Its hair still long and stuck to its body. Its eyes hollow yet still staring at her like pits.

The thing didn't wait as it hurled itself at her with a monstrous wail.

Lucie fell back, her face smashing into the

sideboard. Her nose broke on impact as blood spilled from her nostrils.

Crashing to the carpet, she didn't wait, as she started crawling away, straight razor still in her grasp.

The thing turned to follow her, but did not let her get far before it roared and fell upon her, smashing Lucie with her bony fists, clawing at her skin with her nails.

"Why? I did what you wanted!" Lucie cried out, struggling to free herself as she swung the razor wildly.

The blade cut through the air, but didn't seem to touch her attacker. In an instant, the creature's arm shot out, grabbing Lucie's wrist.

As the three remaining fingers on the creature's ruined hand violently grabbed the razor out of her grip, Lucie's scream changed in nature. From fear to pain.

The blade came down and sliced into Lucie's arm. Chest. Side. Several slashes, each deep, opened up a flow of blood.

As with each one came a cackle. Not from the creature, but from the ceiling above, where staring down at her, the small, crawling boy was in hysterics, watching her being attacked.

Lucie couldn't defend herself; she could only endure it as she tried her best to crawl away.

From her periphery, more horrible things watched.

More twisted and mutilated things. Things that were once people. Now butchered and wrong. All laughing with the skittering boy on the ceiling.

Pulling herself out of the room and out into the hallway, her body became numb as she felt each new slice being met upon her body, but the pain had turned to a chill. She could hear the creature behind her, clambering as it swung the razor into her body. She could hear its raging moans and the others' laughter.

Down the hallway she crawled, wailing and crying, until she saw a half-opened closet up ahead. Scrambling as fast as she could, she managed to make it to the sliding door, hurl herself inside, and slam it shut behind her. Putting all her weight against its frame so it remained closed.

On the other side, the creature didn't wait as it slammed its shoulder against the slatted wood of the door, trying to break its way in.

As Lucie defiantly screamed, bracing her bleeding legs against the wall, keeping the door from opening any more, the bangs slowed until they finally stopped. The laughter and the groans were also dying out.

She screamed once more, expecting a second assault, but it didn't come.

Instead, there was silence, as if nothing had happened.

After a few minutes had passed, and nothing came, Lucie noticed a small box of objects on the floor in front of her. A box of unused items. At the top of them, a small crucifix.

She kept herself blocking the door as she closed her eyes.

"Our Father, who art in heaven, hallowed..." She couldn't remember much more of the prayer. "Hallowed be your... Hallowed..."

Lucie panicked more and focused more on the prayer.

"I beg you, baby Jesus... It's not my fault! I killed the evil. Please... Protect me."

In the silent darkness, Lucie was in a grimy tiled room.

Ten years old, she was strapped to a metal chair, stripped of clothes, filthy, beyond tears, beyond calling for help. She just existed in a cruel space. She had no idea that she was in an old slaughterhouse. All she knew was that she was somewhere filled with pain and torment, manacled to the armrests.

A scratching could be heard on the door. A sound she knew all too well. The sound the monster made before it came. Like the ringing of a bell, the scratching heralded agony.

The door then unlocked and opened.

Lucie couldn't bring herself to look up, but could only whimper at the sound, knowing that the monster who entered was about to hurt her again.

CHAPTER FIVE

THE AFTERMATH

Anna's Renault turned down Allée Jean Baptiste Charlemagne and began to slow as she looked out of the window, taking in the house numbers.

One.

Two.

Three.

Each successive number only made her worry increase.

Four.

Five.

Getting to number six, she pulled into the drive and rolled to a stop on the gravel, behind the family hatchback that was already parked there.

Peering out of her windscreen at the silent house, the rain was spitting down in large drops. The house looked quiet. No lights on. No door open.

Anna started to feel a bit easier, thinking maybe Lucie broke in and just found more evidence.

I'm in their house was what she said.

Killing the engine, Anna opened the door and hesitantly stepped out.

The front door creaked loudly into the hallway as it opened.

"Lucie?" Anna called out.

Only silence replied.

Right then, she could smell it, the metallic tang hanging in the air, as well as another rancid stench.

Walking along the hallway, her shoe trod on something sticky, forcing her to look down. She instantly saw what it was: long spatters of drying blood across the laminate and lying just ahead was Paul Belfond—a gaping wound in his chest.

Everything inside Anna's mind screamed at her to leave.

"Oh god," she whispered as her heart began to pound faster and faster.

"Lucie?" she shouted out in desperation.

She forced herself forward, stepping around the body and looking into the living room. Empty. Then the dining room. Empty.

"Lucie?" she called out again.

Then she walked into the kitchen.

The room was in chaos, with overturned chairs, smashed dishes, and blood everywhere.

Anna clasped a hand over her mouth as she backed up against the wall, seeing the murdered body of

Antoine Belfond in the chair, his brains slopped out of his cracked skull.

"No, no, no," she said, backing up. "*Lucie?*" she now screamed.

Anna looked up at the ceiling, starting to shake with nerves, dreading the prospect of looking upstairs, but knowing she had no choice.

"*Lucie?*" she repeated, running back to the staircase, around Paul's body. "Please answer me?"

She climbed each step, and with each one, she started to lose control a bit more. By the top, she was sobbing.

"Lucie?"

Walking down the hallway, she heard it, crying from the open closet.

The door was half slid across, and Lucie lay inside, covered in deep cuts, from her face to her ankles.

Anna knelt at the door. Reaching out, she touched Lucie's shoulder. As she did, Lucie suddenly shrieked in terror.

"It's me, Lucie! It's Anna, please!"

Lucie struggled to return to reality as she stared up at Anna in disbelief.

"It's me! Calm down!"

Slowly, Anna's shocked expression disappeared. "Anna?"

"It's okay, I'm here. I'm here."

Lucie looked suddenly fearful as she sat up and peered into the hallway, then back to Anna. "She's here! She's in the house!" she said, whispering, before starting to cry more.

"Shhh, it's okay." Anna tried to quell her tears so she could be strong for Lucie, but they were both crying with little control.

"She hurt me again." Lucie's head dropped as she hunched over, grabbing her knees.

Anna leaned in and hugged her, and as she did, she saw the extent of the cuts. The very deep and wide cuts.

"Shit, these don't look good." Thinking for a moment, Anna looked around. "Stay here, okay?"

But Lucie's hand stopped her, grabbing her by the wrist.

"Don't leave me!"

With a sympathetic smile, Anna stroked Lucie's cheek.

"You'll be safe here."

"No," Lucie pleaded.

"I *have* to go see. Stay here."

Under Lucie's worried gaze, Anna stood up and opened the other doors in the hallway.

Finding the bathroom, she looked in the cabinet. It was empty.

Rushing back downstairs, she was desperately trying to piece together what had happened.

Skirting around Paul, avoiding looking at his dead-eyed stare, she walked back into the kitchen and again saw Antoine's body at the kitchen table.

Taking a few steps further, she then noticed the further extent of the slaughter.

The bodies, soaked in their own dark blood. Murdered at lunch.

Anna put her hand to her mouth and shook her head, walking back out of the kitchen and into the living room.

There on the carpet was the murder weapon. The shotgun.

As Anna's eyes welled with tears again, she soon felt a presence behind her.

Lucie was there in the hallway, beside Paul Belfond's body, looking in at her with an innocent gaze. Her hand gripping the bloody straight razor.

"I don't want to be alone," she whispered.

Anna nodded, but was on the verge of losing all her composure. She tried to smile as she walked out of the room and into the downstairs bathroom. She shut the door behind her, locking it. Despite the enormous effort to contain herself, she could not hold her emotions inside any longer.

She turned the faucet on full to cover the sounds of her upset.

Outside, Lucie was now at the door, trying the handle.

"Anna?" she said.

Anna didn't answer, as her emotional breakdown seized her.

"She found me. I don't know how," Lucie

continued, sounding like when she was ten. "She hurt me even more…"

At the sink, Anna put her head under the stream of cold water.

"Anna, please. I need you."

Lucie started to turn the door handle more insistently, but the lock kept her out.

Having to push everything inside, Anna wiped her face and looked into the mirror at her reflection. "I… I'm coming," she called out. "One minute, okay?"

"What am I going to do?" Lucie asked.

Anna tried to be calm. To think about what to do.

She could see it now. A collection of police officers grabbing Lucie and dragging her out of the house without mercy, then throwing her into the police van. She would struggle, scream for Anna pleadingly. And Anna would be standing there on the porch of the house, watching her leave. Having condemned her best friend to a newer hell.

No. That couldn't happen.

Opening the bathroom cabinet, she found what she needed. A first aid kit. Grabbing it, she opened the bathroom door, expecting Lucie to be there. Instead, she had moved into the living room, the shotgun picked up, looking it over.

"I ran out of cartridges," Lucie said, not looking up.

Anna ignored this. "Come on. Upstairs."

Looking shocked, Lucie looked at her. "Upstairs? What? Why don't we just leave?"

"Come on," Anna urged, holding up the first aid box.

"But she'll come back!"

Lucie's protest was met with silence as Anna trod up the staircase, needing to be as far from the violence as she could be in here.

Lucie sat on the bed of the master bedroom, her shirt off, as Anna dressed and cleaned the wounds over her body.

Her skin was a roadmap of suffering. Her shoulder blades, arms, neck, hips, and breasts were entirely covered with horrifying scars, not only from what she endured as a child but also over the years. Now, there was also a broken nose, fresh bruises, as well as the razor blade slashes.

With a tissue soaked in antiseptic, Anna cleaned the last of her open wounds. Some definitely needed stitches, but there was nothing she could do about that now.

"Your nose looks broken," Anna said. "Might have to have a doctor look at it."

"They won't put me in prison, will they?" Lucie asked, too preoccupied to care about her body's damage.

Anna shrugged, dabbing the ointment onto the cleaned cuts.

Lucie struggled to find the words. "If I... If I... get sent to an asylum, I think I'd die there."

"You won't go there," Anna said. "I'm not going to allow that."

But Lucie wasn't listening. "They send all the crazies there, and that's what I am, aren't I? You think I am."

"I said I won't let them take you."

Lucie nodded. "If you weren't here, I'd..." Her words faltered. Hating the very idea.

"Why did you do this, Lucie?" Anna asked, finally looking up at her. She wanted to shout at her, to shake Lucie hard, to smack some sense into her, but had to hold herself back.

Lucie looked at her with a strange curiosity. "I told you. They're the ones," came her hollow reply.

"Lucie, you killed a *family*? You do understand that, don't you?"

"No. They're *not* a family," Lucie snapped back, shaking her head. "It was *them*. The ones who hurt me. They are *devils*. They are *filth*."

"You don't *know* that, Lucie. You *can't* know it was them."

Lucie grabbed onto Anna's arm. "I *remember*, Anna. I remember it all. I remember *her*. I can't ever forget it."

Anna pulled herself free. "Then you should have called the police like we agreed, not this. *Not this!*"

"You don't believe me, do you?"

But Anna couldn't answer that, not without hurting her. She gathered her thoughts as quickly as she could.

"Lucie," she said, with a stern look. "We can't leave. We have to clean this up, okay?" she said. "We have to make it so no one can say you were here. I said I'll protect you, and that's exactly what I'll do. We spent all day at home. All day together."

Lucie was wide-eyed, listening.

"Do you understand what I'm saying?" Anna asked.

Lucie nodded, though unconvincingly.

"Well, come on. Get dressed."

The rain outside began weakening, and the sun took over for a short time, throwing its rays down upon the Belfond house. Through the kitchen window, the golden beams shone upon the murdered family.

One by one, the bodies were dragged from where they fell and taken into the downstairs bathroom, piled in the tile-lined shower. Anna had to close her eyes as she carried, Lucie did so without complaint or even seeming bothered about what they were doing.

"I hope they're in hell," she mumbled as she stared at the dead eyes of Gabrielle, who looked back at her from the bottom of the pile of corpses.

Anna, meanwhile, could not stomach any more of it and vomited into the toilet. Without any food in her belly, it was just bile that burned her throat, and heaving that stung her belly.

"What's wrong?" Lucie asked. "Are you ill?"

Anna waved her hand, motioning for Lucie to leave her alone.

Nodding with worry, Lucie complied and walked out of the room, only to return a few seconds later.

"It disgusts you, doesn't it?" she said, with some annoyance.

But Anna couldn't reply as she was retching again.

Lucie's tone suddenly became angrier. "Is that it? It disgusts you? I disgust you?"

"No," Anna managed to gasp, but seeing the bodies in her periphery, she could not stop herself from retching once more.

Lucie shook her head and walked over to the corpses. She crouched in front of them and stared at the mother. She seized her lolling arm and yanked it up to her face, smelling the inside of her wrist.

"That smell," she snarled, dropping it down and turning back to Anna. "That smell. That filthy fucking smell!"

Anna, pale as a sheet, looked over, unsure of what to say.

"I smelled that same perfume every time she leaned over me! *Every* time, do you understand what I'm saying? When she beat me! Cut me! *That's* what I smelled. *That* smell! And I had to look at her face the whole time."

Anna nodded, not wanting to enrage her anymore.

"And you think I'm too stupid to recognize them? Because it was a long time ago? Because I was a child?"

Anna wiped her mouth, woozy as she replied weakly, "No. I didn't mean that. Just... this..."

Lucie got up and reached into her back pocket, pulling out the newspaper cutting and holding it up with contempt in Anna's direction.

"It's them! No ifs or buts. *THEM!*"

Later, Anna was in the hallway. The smell of bleach extinguished the stench of blood; the rug beneath her knees was sodden yet still stained red where the blood had dripped out of Paul. She had tried scrubbing hard, but the tinge of blood was too stubborn to leave. She would have to get rid of it. Rolling it up, she propped it up against the wall, then grabbed the mop to clean the damp floorboards beneath. After having vomited and cried all she could, Anna met this work with cold detachment.

Lucie was on the couch, calm and happy, like someone waiting for a bus. She watched Anna cleaning without making any comment.

But when Anna looked back and saw her stare, Lucie felt like she had to say something.

"I swear to you it was them," she said.

"Yeah," was all Anna could say before moving her cleaning into the kitchen, leaving Lucie alone.

She tried to stay where she was, but as she stood up, she went to follow Anna, only to see the bathroom door open, beckoning her.

Walking in, she was met once more with the sight of the Belfonds' remains at the foot of the shower.

Lucie glared hatefully at them. She got to her haunches and glared closely at Gabrielle's slack-jawed face.

"You hear me?" Lucie whispered. "I hope you rot for what you did."

Feeling victorious, she laughed. Looking at each body in turn.

"Filth making filth making filth," she murmured. "Evil making evil making evil."

She stood up to walk out to see Anna. Instead, something shifted in the room. In her head. A whisper of breath that didn't come from her mouth, but from the shower.

She stopped and slowly turned.

At the bottom of the pile, Gabrielle's mouth twitched.

The twitch then became a smirk, then a bloody, wide, sneering grin.

Lucie shook her head hard, backing away.

Gabrielle's smile widened even more.

"You can't win," the dead woman said, her voice too loud for her dead throat, too loud for anything human. The sound made Lucie's ears sting.

She backed away to the wall, trembling, and the bodies shifted again—not with movement, but with attention.

Paul's head turned around, his neck bones breaking as he faced her.

Marie's eyes rolled toward her.

The remaining half of Antoine's head also glared impossibly at attention.

Then all four grinned the same grin as they said in absolute unison:

"You lost."

The word didn't sound in the bathroom.

They echoed within Lucie.

"You lost. You lost. You lost," they chanted, their mouths sadistically gleeful.

Lucie shut her eyes tight and gripped her head. "No. You're dead," she said through gritted teeth. "Dead. Dead. Dead!"

As she then screamed, the sound didn't block their mockery. It only made room for them to crawl deeper into her psyche.

Anna heard and ran back into the bathroom.

She found Lucie hunched in a corner, staring at the bodies, yelling uncontrollably about how they had just spoken to her.

"They can't win... They can't win..." she kept repeating,

After Anna moved her back to the master bedroom, Lucie eventually wore herself out and fell asleep.

.   .   .

An hour later, dark clouds thickened over the neighborhood again, blotting out the daylight that dared to peek through; the rain returned in full force.

Anna was in the kitchen, with a numbness wrapped around her.

On her knees with a sponge in her hand, that numbness was disappearing, and the reality of what she was doing was seeping in through the cracks.

The floor was sticky. Not wet the way she expected, but the blood had congealed. As Anna wiped the sponge through it, she immediately felt the tacky resistance of that liquid that once circulated inside a living human.

She swallowed hard and kept wiping. But the longer she was there, the more the room revealed its former life to her. She found fragments that weren't gore, but shards of a plate, the crust of a sandwich, and a hair tie. Every time she picked out something ordinary, the horror of it doubled. Somehow, the mundane was more unbearable to find than the violence.

This family had eaten here. Then minutes later, they were just... gone.

Her gaze moved to the refrigerator. There was a family photo pinned by a magnet. Everyone making silly faces to the camera.

A gasping sound escaped her mouth as she forced herself to turn back and scrub harder.

Her determination was focused as if making this

room clean would clean the past. Make Lucie clean again.

The sponge then slipped from her grip. When she picked it back up, a piece of something soft clung to it. Something gray-pink, spongy, with a texture she recognized instantly from the hospital.

Brain tissue.

She steadied herself against the counter next to her, fighting the surge of bile inside.

This wasn't just Lucie's crime scene, now. Now Anna saw herself as a willing participant, simply by trying to save her friend.

"I can't do this," she whispered.

But she had to carry on and view it all as clinically as possible.

It was meat.

Meat.

Meat that needed disposing of.

She had a plan, but had no idea how realistic it was.

Night was in full force when Lucie eventually woke in the master bedroom.

Sitting up, she heard the rain battering the window, joined by the far rumble of thunder.

Looking down at herself, she noticed she was in underwear and a clean T-shirt. Her bloody clothes now neatly folded on a chair beside the bed.

Getting to her feet, she walked to the door and peeked worriedly out into the hallway. There was nothing there, but not seeing anything wasn't good enough.

She closed the door, grabbed the chair, and wedged it against the door handle to stop it from opening.

Picking up her clothes, she looked through the pockets and, finding what she was looking for, took out the straight razor.

Anna was no longer in the kitchen, but outside in the dark, in the pouring rain. She had gone to the edge of the backyard, where the woodland opened up, and started digging with a shovel she had found in the garage.

The hole she had made was large and deep, and it soon became a muddy pit.

Dragging the body of Antoine Belfond across the rain-sodden lawn, she didn't look at him, just keeping her view around her, making sure no one was watching.

When she got to the edge of the makeshift grave, she didn't waste any more time as she hauled Antoine's limp remains inside. His body tumbled into the hole where another body had already been thrown: his father, Paul.

Seeing them lying together, Anna was still unable to come to terms with what Lucie had done, but she had no other choice but to carry on.

Turning, she started to walk back through the

deluge, toward the house, when she saw her. Lucie, up in the master bedroom window, through a gap in the curtains, looking down at her with a happy smile.

Getting back in, dripping wet, Anna returned to the downstairs bathroom, where the other two corpses waited to be taken.

She had already been working for hours, and her body was aching. She was beyond exhausted and running on fumes. Mud and blood caked her body, and as she looked in the mirror, she barely recognized the woman staring back.

She walked over to the sink, turned on the faucet, and splashed water onto her face, rubbing off the dirt. Then, she took a breath and got back to the matter at hand.

She had moved the heaviest bodies; now it should be easier, and by the next morning, it would all be over.

Marie's body had been dragged to the door, waiting to be taken to the grave next, with Gabrielle still slumped in the shower. Anna knelt in front of Marie, grabbing her shoulder, ready to lift. But as she did, a sound made her suddenly drop the body in fright.

A wheeze.

Anna didn't know where the sound came from, but when she turned, it made her scurry back in fear.

It was Gabrielle, with her eyes open. Not staring in any blank death, but alive and looking directly at Anna.

Blood sloughed from her mouth as she spoke. Her voice was no more than a gurgle. She weakly reached for Anna.

"Help..." was all she could manage.

For a moment, Anna could only stare in shock until Gabrielle let out a pained cry, one that mixed in with the thunder rolling high above.

Lucie was sitting in the master bedroom when she heard that sound. She wasn't sure what it was, but knew that it came from downstairs.

The mother's pained moans continued, as Anna panicked, wondering what she should do.

"Anna?" came a call from upstairs. *"Is that you?"*

Staring at the anguished woman, Anna tried to think fast.

"My... children," Gabrielle sobbed in confusion and pain.

"Anna!" Lucie's second call came more urgently. *"Can you hear me?"*

In the hallway above, Lucie had walked out of the room, straight razor in hand, and looked to the staircase, worried.

"Anna?"

· · ·

Gabrielle uttered another cry, one of despair as she remembered what had happened.

"Anna, what are you doing?" Lucie called out, getting to the stairs.

Looking at the mother, Anna knew she had to decide what to do and do it fast.

As Lucie got to the ground floor, razor held out, she saw the bathroom door opening, and Anna walk out, dragging Marie's body behind her.

Reassured, Lucie lowered the blade.

"Are you okay?" she asked. "Why didn't you answer me?"

"Sorry, I was in the bathroom washing my face. I couldn't hear you," Anna lied.

"I thought... I thought she'd come back."

Anna couldn't meet her gaze. "No, just gotta bury this one, then the mother, then fill the hole."

"And after that, we can leave?" Lucie said hopefully.

"Yeah, just gotta do one final mop of the floor... So, you may as well go get dressed, okay?"

With an excited smile, Lucie turned and ran back upstairs.

Across the lawn, Anna dragged Marie's small body, but even at her size, her dead weight was getting too much.

Struggling to keep balance on increasingly muddy ground, Anna stumbled, letting go of Marie's arms into the mud.

At the end of her will, Anna felt like she should just run to her car. Drive away. Never look back. But before that thought could take any real hold, something drew her attention back to the master bedroom window.

The thunder boomed as a shadow shifted behind the curtain. Then, with an almighty crash, it slammed into the glass. Shards broke out, falling to the ground, as the curtain rail collapsed with it. Through the jagged opening, Lucie's blood-covered face appeared, screaming.

Anna ran through the back door, into the kitchen, and up the stairs.

"Lucie!" she screamed, feeling that tonight was on constant repeat.

As she hurried down the length of the hallway and looked into the master bedroom. There was nobody— just the shattered window.

"Lucie?" she shouted again.

"I'm in here," came the sad reply, coming from the en-suite. From behind the closed door.

Anna walked over, turned the handle, but it was locked.

"Lucie?"

"Open the door," replied the voice.

"I can't, it's locked," Anna tried the handle again.

"Open," Lucie repeated. "Please open the door."

"I can't. It's locked..."

"Open the door," Lucie said again. "Please, I'll do what you want!"

Anna then realized that Lucie wasn't talking to her.

The sound of a heavy thump and a cry of pain followed, and Lucie let out a loud wail.

On her stomach in the middle of the en-suite. Lucie's clothes were newly slashed, her nose bleeding heavily again.

Terrified, she didn't want to look up, but she was unable to ignore it. She could hear the moans coming from it; she knew the creature was there.

The emaciated thing was crouched in a corner of the bathroom, its back now turned to her, and in its grasp it held the straight razor.

It turned its empty-eyed glare around and stared at her.

In the surreal chiaroscuro of the small room, the creature grinned as it held the blade out and brought it down onto its own bare chest. It was a vision of self-mutilation as it cut through the multitude of scars and sores already covering its skin.

And as it cut, a liquid seeped out. Black and thick like oil, it dripped with each new laceration.

The sounds the creature made were like a cracked

sexual moan, as the razor sliced into its skin, then out again.

Over and over, she dug the blade in. Penetrating its flesh in a perverse rhythm. And each moan sounded more and more pleasurable.

The razor sliced over its groin, belly, breasts, until it approached her neck.

Pausing the moan, the creature let out a giggle. A horrible sound. As the razor found the carotid.

Turning away from the horror, Lucie, bleeding heavily, crawled to the door. But there was the boy, skittering on all fours, laughing.

Which only made the others laugh as well. All appearing around the small room and staring down at her.

Anna kicked the bathroom door, trying to break it open, but it was a heavy slab of wood, and the lock was firmly in place.

The creature, hunched, spread-legged in the corner, laughing a malevolent sneer, before launching toward Lucie again for another round.

Anna slammed herself into the door, nearly dislocating her shoulder as she collided. Again and again she hit herself into it, until the wood finally started to crack.

. . .

Lucie managed to stagger to her feet, dripping blood on the floor in thick ropes.

Anna slammed herself one more time against the door, and it finally gave in. The wood split down the middle and tore out of the lock's grasp.

Before she could see anything, Anna felt a hand grab hers, and Lucie burst out of the bathroom, dragging her out of the room into the hallway. But as she did, Anna's feet stumbled and she tripped forward.

As Lucie turned to help her up, a furious howl from the bathroom made her look back. There the creature stood, with an insane grin on its face, razor in hand, with its dark blood spraying from its wounds.

"Quick," Lucie bellowed as she helped Anna up again and resumed running away.

With the creature running fast, gaining with each step, Lucie pulled Anna into Marie's bedroom.

Turning the key in the lock, she then pushed Anna back as she shouted to the thing in the hallway.

"I killed them!" she yelled.

"Please, Lucie, calm down," Anna said, scared as she witnessed.

"Even the kids. I killed them for you! What more do you want?"

That made Anna stop. *For you?*

Lucie continued, "Please leave me alone, haven't I done enough?"

Anna looked around the room. At the mess that Lucie had caused earlier. She saw the remains of Marie's life. The dresser, covered in heart-shaped stickers, and the posters on the walls. A series of photographs stuck to the edges of the mirror... A baby Marie posing in one. Another of her parents. One of her was with an old lady, presumably her grandmother. One of her brother. One of the family all together on holiday.

Outside, the storm raged more and more, and as it reached a crescendo... Blackout.

Everything went dark... for Lucie.

The light of a gas lamp lit ten-year-old Lucie's pale, beaten face as she sat on the edge of the mattress. The battering she had been given had swollen her cheek and eye, as her lip dripped blood from where it had been split.

She sat there, looking forward, as next to her, her torturer sat. A woman whom Lucie was not allowed to look at. If she did, there would be an immediate and brutal punishment.

The woman held a bowl of rancid gruel in her hand and a heaped wooden spoon in the other.

Lucie was not strong enough to resist, as the foul food was forced between her teeth. She choked on the taste, coughing it back up onto the floor.

The woman's temper soon flared, as her hand came down, slapping her hard on the back of the head.

Lucie then broke the other rule; she made a sound. She had screamed in pain.

The woman threw the bowl on the floor and grabbed Lucie's manacles. Unlocking them by the clasps. Ready to drag her back to the metal chair.

But as she did, the young Lucie struggled in panic, knowing what was coming.

Gripped by fury, the woman threw the chains to the floor, but was too slow to stop Lucie pulling her arms away. A move she didn't expect after over a year of keeping this girl in battered line.

Lucie quickly got to her feet and pushed the woman back. She stumbled and tripped over the metal ring fixed in the floor. The ring that held the chains in place.

As the woman fell, she turned to brace herself against the ground. But her knee hit the concrete with a heavy force, and the crack that came from her patella made her howl.

Disoriented, Lucie quickly realized that the door to the room had been left open. The woman noticed it too, which added more rage to her pain. She doubled her screams at Lucie, not in words, but just as a primal noise.

She crawled after the girl, desperately trying to stop her running despite the pain, but Lucie had already run out, slamming the door shut behind her.

Lucie raced away, but her panic sent her direction

askew. She didn't know which way to go, and checked every door she came to.

The ones she peered into were all empty rooms, until she got to one that wasn't.

When she opened that door, she heard a moan. A moan of agony. A moan she had heard many times through the walls since being brought here.

In a recess of the damp, squalid space, a woman had been held prisoner in the same way as Lucie had. Sitting in the same sort of hole-riddled chair, with the same kinds of restraints.

Her body was entirely covered with cuts, bruises, welts, and sores, testifying to the even more horrible torments than Lucie had so far endured. From head to toe, this poor victim was nothing but a field of macabre cruelty. Her eyes had been carved out, and she just had two large pits that glared forward.

Sensing Lucie there, the moan came from behind the woman's sewn-up mouth.

Despite the chains, despite the exhaustion, she tried to call out.

Even without words, Lucie could sense the woman pleading for help. But she didn't know what she could do. Her tormentor was only in the other room.

The tortured girl increased her pleading groans.

Lucie looked back into the corridor and saw a man, having heard the commotion, coming out of one of the rooms. He was dressed like a butcher, in a mask, apron, and rubber gloves... He quickly moved to Lucie's room, hearing the woman's angry screams from within, and opened the door.

Lucie had no thoughts left except saving her own life, so she turned and ran.

It was a painful, almost impossible escape, as her legs were so weak. She stumbled many times down the winding corridors, trying to find the exit. And each time she did, she got back up, not letting herself stop.

Getting to a wider room, she saw a painted arrow on the wall in front of her. The word EXIT in large letters above it. This word pushed her to carry on.

She soon reached the double doors and pushed with all her might.

As she did, the sunlight cascaded in, and she ran. Ran to the road and did not stop until she couldn't run anymore.

Lucie awoke, shaking off the images that plagued her mind, feeling as though it all had happened only yesterday.

She was on the carpet. Face down.

She looked around, having no idea of what had happened. They were being chased, they came in here, then... nothing. She then felt a sharp pain in her head.

"Anna?" she said weakly, but she quickly realized that she was alone in Marie's bedroom.

Confused, she got to her feet and walked to the door with worried steps.

She went to unlock it, but the key was gone.

"Anna?" she asked again.

No answer came, and she immediately panicked.

"*Anna!*"

From the downstairs bathroom, Anna walked out. With one arm around the still-alive Gabrielle, she carried her into the hallway.

The mother had no strength left and had nearly bled out. Her eyes fluttered as she stood on the precipice of consciousness. Anna took as much weight as she could and staggered forward.

"Stay with me," Anna said, dragging her along. "Tell me your name!"

"Gabrielle," came the spluttered reply.

Upstairs, Lucie was more panicked.

"Anna! Anna!" she screamed. "Please, don't leave me! Anna!"

"*Anna!*" came louder from upstairs.

Anna looked over her shoulder at the staircase. "I'm coming, Lucie!" she shouted.

Gabrielle held on, but through her pain and suffering, she was also livid with the memory of what happened.

"Why... Did...She... Do... This," Gabrielle gasped, in agony.

Anna was more concerned about getting the woman away from the scene than answering questions, so she headed to the back door. "Look, you're going to have to help me here, Gabrielle, understand?"

"Call an ambulance," Gabriel pleaded, almost slipping from her own sanity, at the same time as Anna's grasp. "For my children. They need a hospital."

Anna slowed as she looked to the woman, unable not to ask the one burning question in her mind. "Tell me... Fifteen years ago, did you kidnap a small girl?"

But Gabrielle was not in any fit state to comprehend the question. She just stared at her in pain. "Help my children," she moaned.

Anna shook off the worry, turning back to walk through the kitchen. "We have to go. Hurry."

"Ambulance," Gabrielle repeated. "*Please!*"

"I'll get to the woods, then you're on your own."

Through the window, the black expanse of the backyard and forest could be seen.

They were both in too much panic to hear Lucie break out of the room above and rush down after them.

She appeared from behind and barged into the mother, knocking her out of Anna's grasp.

The woman fell hard onto the floor.

Lucie stared as the woman collapsed and stopped, her gaze fixed on the back of her jumper.

There was only one shotgun wound, across her midsection.

Lucie *swore* that she shot the woman many times. She remembered standing over her in the utility room and pulling the trigger. She remembered the back of her head after the shot burst through it.

Now... none of that was here.

As the woman whined in pain, turning to look up. Lucie's face fell to pure hatred.

Anna had no time to stop anything as Lucie rushed over to the counter, to the open toolbox on the floor, and grabbed the first thing she could; the hammer.

Immediately, she slammed it onto Gabrielle's face. But the attack didn't stop there.

She kept going.

Harder and harder she hit the hammer onto the woman.

Gabrielle's pleas for help were short-lived as her face cracked in. Her teeth were smashed first, as she tried to cry out, and then her jaw was bashed off. The next hammer blows burst her eyeballs, and the sockets soon shattered. Her skull was then pulverized until it hit the brain.

"Stop!" Anna begged, but it was already far too late.

The hammer kept going, Lucie kept screaming in anguish, brutally destroying the woman in front of her. The woman she would have sworn that she had already killed.

"Lucie, please!" Anna cried, grabbing Lucie by the shoulders to pull her away, but Lucie was uncontrollable.

As Gabrielle's head became just a pit of mush, with

no visible trace of her face left, Anna managed to grab Lucie by the waist and yank her backward.

Lucie screamed angrily and lashed out. She swung the hammer at Anna, hitting her on the side of the head, sending her staggering out of the room and dazing her.

Outside, the storm had turned up a notch, as the rain came down like bullets, and the thunder brought with it vast sheets of lightning.

The weather now matched chaos inside, as Lucie got to her feet.

She was now in a blind rampage. Her expression has never looked so hateful as she turned to Anna, who staggered through the hallway and into the living room, grabbing her bleeding temple with one hand.

For the first time since they met, Anna was scared of her friend.

"That's why she was still in the house," Lucie hatefully shouted, as she pointed with the hammer back to Gabrielle's dead body. "Because that cunt wasn't gone! I thought she was, but I was wrong." She then turned the bloody hammer on Anna. "And you, you wanted to save her!"

Anna cried as she pleaded. "Lucie, she didn't do anything. None of them did. It's all in your head! It's not real."

"She hurt me! *Me!*" Lucie swiped the hammer in the air as she spoke. "She did it, and you're on her side. You wanted that devil to live! But I stopped it. I stopped it all!"

"Lucie!" Anna begged, he legs buckling as she fell to the carpet. Her vision off balance, and swirling.

But she was seized by an anger beyond anything Anna had witnessed in her life.

"You *never* believed me!" she said, her voice breaking with upset.

"I'm on your side!" Anna protested, doing her best to back away across the floor.

"NO! You think I'm crazy. Just like the others do."

Furiously, Lucie swung the hammer into a mirror on the wall. It smashed on impact, sending shards across the room.

"I'm alone now... And you're against me, right? You of all people."

"Don't," Anna managed to say, but Lucie's attention moved.

She saw a collection of family photos on the sideboard. All smiling out at her.

"Fuck you!" Lucie yelled as she raised the hammer and smashed the frames with repeated hammer blows, pummeling them onto the wood of the sideboard. All but one fell to the floor: a smiling photo of Gabrielle Belfond.

At the sight of her smiling face, Lucie saw it as mocking.

She then swung the hammer as hard as she could, and it came crashing down through the frame.

The picture was destroyed as the hammer embedded through her face, just as it had been in real life.

The hammer remained in the sideboard, embedded through the frame, and into the wood.

Lucie saw this and let out a half-cruel, half-devastated laugh.

"Stop!" Anna was pleading as she staggered upright, her vision a total blur, with blood trickling down her cheek. She blinked hard, trying to get some focus, and when she did, it was just in time to see a change in Lucie.

The rage had immediately left her face.

Her laugh had died out.

She was staring out of the room, at the staircase, mouth open in shock.

"How..." she said.

Anna turned to follow her gaze, but despite seeing nothing, she knew what Lucie was seeing.

Lucie then glanced out through the hallway, into the kitchen and saw Gabrielle's lifeless body. As she did, she finally came to understand. Nothing, absolutely nothing, would ever make the creature leave.

"Don't look at her," Anna said. "She's in your head. You can ignore her."

But Lucie was not listening.

"Don't look at her!"

There, the creature walked down the stairs, looking at her, carrying the straight razor in its hand.

Lucie searched her pockets to find anything to protect herself.

She brought out the same straight razor from her pocket—the same one the creature now held.

Walking closer, Lucie closed her eyes and smiled, as a lucid moment took hold. The rage, the mania cleared for a beat.

"I love you, Anna," she said, as the creature rushed toward her, razor wielded high.

In her eyes, the creature attacked, pushing her to the floor, and in a wild frenzy delivered dozens of bloody blows. Slashing at her with the razor. In her eyes, she called for Anna's help. In her eyes, she did all she could to survive.

Anna stood by, helpless.

Lucie was on the floor. Silent, as she held the razor in her hand, and one after the other cut into her own flesh. Not screaming and not crying, and just breathing shallow and mutilating herself.

In Lucie's eyes, the creature carried on slashing and slashing.

In reality, she kept on slashing herself.

"Tell her to stop," Lucie wheezed, with an expressionless face, cutting into herself repeatedly. "Tell her.... please. Tell her."

In Lucie's eyes, the creature wouldn't stop. And she tried her best to escape.

Forcing herself to her feet, she carried on slicing at her body as she staggered down the hallway toward the large windows in the living room.

Thinking only of running, she screamed.

In her eyes, the creature was rushing around her. *Slice. Slice. Slice.*

With a deliberate effort, Anna pushed aside her pain and hobbled after her. But the dizziness in her eyes persisted, and the room around her started to spin. The hammer to the head left a lot more damage than she thought.

But she carried on, not thinking of herself, only of Lucie.

The floor-to-ceiling windows leading onto the front porch smashed outward as Lucie fell through. She rolled through the shards, across the porch, and landed in a bloody heap on the muddy lawn.

In her eyes, the creature leapt out after and carried on its assault.

In reality, she carried it on cutting herself. *Slice. Slice. Slice.*

She lay, her body a mass of damaged flesh.

And then, she stopped.

The creature stopped. As it stared down at her, it wondered if she was still alive, or if she had already died.

The rain beat down hard, instantly washing her blood into the ground below.

The creature smiled as it bent down over her.

Anna finally reached the porch and saw Lucie struggling on her own in the mud.

Lucie didn't see her friend staring helplessly in abject horror. She was too busy trying to free herself from the grip of the creature above. But the creature was too strong.

Leaning down, it held the razor tight, ready for the final cut.

Anna could only watch as Lucie raised the razor to her throat.

One last slice.

The cut was quick, the artery severed. The blood pumped out along with the pulse of her dying heart.

Anna ran over as fast as she could, collapsing beside her. She immediately tried to stem the bleeding from Lucie's neck, pressing the wound with her palm, but too much blood had already left her body.

"Please, hold on. Please, please, please," she begged.

But Lucie's glassy eyes just stared out, the life already gone from them.

When Anna finally noticed, she moved her hand away and gathered Lucie into her arms, cradling her as the tears choked her cries.

CHAPTER SIX

GOODBYE

As the clock struck 6 p.m., the sun was buried behind the storm and began to set, deepening the gloom toward night.

The rain had kept on falling, washing all trace of Lucie's blood into the earth below the blades of grass.

Now her body lay rolled in a bedsheet on the living room floor. Wrapped in a shroud, only her face was showing. Her body had been cleaned, the cuts across her now barely visible. She looked pale, innocent, and beautiful.

The rest of the house was as it had been. So much of the violence had been cleaned up, yet new violence sat in its place. Marie remained lying on the back lawn. Paul and Antoine lay piled in their open grave. Gabrielle, with her pulped head, was still a mess in the kitchen.

Anna didn't know what to do. Should she take

Lucie's body somewhere? Leave it here and wait for the detectives to work out the events?

Picking up the telephone, she had intended to call the police, but instead called another number.

"Hello, Mom?"

"It's about damn time!" the impatient voice on the other end said. *"The hospital called, you didn't show up for work yesterday or today! Where the bloody hell are you? What are you doing?"*

" I-I'm sorry," Anna replied sadly.

"Your uncle's furious with you. He called in a lot of favors to get you that job! Try finding another one with that kind of wage. Do you even realize how good you have it?"

"Yes, Mom." Even though her mother was furious with her, screaming down the phone, Anna was so happy to hear her voice. Despite the abuse she suffered from her family, it was a familiar thing. It was a normal thing. And Anna desperately needed normality of any kind.

She stared ahead as she spoke, and did not see the hammer in the sideboard begin to move. Lucie's fury had badly damaged the planks of wood that made up the unit's top, and now started to creak, slowly splitting along its length.

"What am I supposed to tell them, Annabelle? I don't even know where you are! I don't know what you're doing! You never tell me anything! So what can I possibly say? I'm not going to lie... I was so embarrassed!"

"I'll call them."

Her mother's tone shifted as she realized that Anna was not arguing back as she usually would.

"Are you okay? Is everything alright?"

Holding back the tears, Anna replied quietly. "Yes."

"Are you sure? It worries me when you disappear like that! You haven't done that in years. Where are you, anyway?"

"Not close."

The sideboard continued to creak quietly. The crack in which the hammer had been embedded now widened as the wood began to move.

Anna noticed but paid it little attention.

"You're with her, aren't you? She's the one making you do all this! As she always does."

"No..."

The hammer slipped deeper into the sideboard.

"You are such a liar! You're with her now, I bet!"

Anna started to cry, seeing Lucie in her shroud out of the corner of her eye.

The hammer kept slipping.

"Good God! It's always the same thing!"

"Mom..."

The wood of the sideboard cracked loudly as the hammer fell inside.

"That girl, Anna... she's no good at all, you need to—"

The sound caused by the hammer's landing came far, far too late. Four long seconds.

It made a strange, metallic impact that echoed loudly, resonating throughout the sideboard and shaking the split wooden top.

It stunned Anna into dropping the phone to the floor.

"Hello?" Came the mother's voice. *"Hello? Hello? Urgh, stupid child."*

But Anna was not paying any attention to anything other than the sideboard.

The line cut to a busy signal as her mother hung up the line with an exasperated sigh.

Anna stepped cautiously over to the sideboard, peering inside its broken top and seeing the dark nothing that lay below.

With a long crack now splitting it, the sideboard's top came off easily. The back of it still attached on hinges—this whole top was a lid. A secret lid.

The darkness within stretched beyond the bottom of the unit, extending even to the floor.

It exposed a hidden metal staircase that led down to a lower level.

A secret basement.

Stepping back, she looked over the sideboard, examining all its surfaces, and noticed that one panel was also hinged. It swung outward, opening her way to whatever was below.

"What the hell?" she whispered.

As she looked down, trying to see in the dark, a wash of cold air rushed out to her. Air that stank of bleach, covering a far worse smell.

A few steps down, she noticed a flashlight hanging from a hook on the wall. Stepping past the hidden entrance and onto the first stair, she reached out and grabbed it. She switched it on and aimed the beam downward.

The metal grating of the steps descended, and the stark white walls made the place feel more like a factory than a suburban home.

Armed with the flashlight, Anna continued into the basement, slowly descending the metal staircase until she reached a long corridor at the bottom.

The beam revealed a rack to her right lined with dozens of wine bottles. Beside it on the wall was a single switch.

Flicking it on, a yellowing light bulb snapped to life. Instead of brightening up the space, it made it look less inviting and murkier with its jaundiced glow.

Anna imagined this was possibly some kind of personal bunker. Maybe the family were survivalists, preparing for the end of times. She had seen documentaries about people like that. Not that she could blame or mock anyone for doing that. With the world as crazy as it was, having a bunker would be different but kind of logical. And that made her even more curious.

As she walked on, the wall on the left took her by surprise. There, hung on the wall, was a gallery of framed photographs.

Not of the family.

Not of friends.

Some were old, damaged by the passing of decades, and others seemed to have been taken more recently. They appeared as if they had come from many cultures across many eras. And in each photo was the same thing: a woman's face.

From one image to the next, the expressions were eerily similar: A calm yet frozen look. With both eyes turned toward the sky, and a strange, slight smile. Like Renaissance paintings of Jesus on the Cross, looking skyward to his father, but these were real and looked far from religious.

However, when she reached some of the pictures further along, the expression became clearer. One photo showed a Chinese peasant woman from the start of the century. Her body had literally been cut to pieces in the middle of a laughing crowd. The grain and sepia tone made it somehow even more terrifying than it already was. Anna didn't want to, but she took a closer look. Despite the torment of the victim, she carried that same look as the other.

The next image, more recent and in color, showed a close-up of a hospital patient on her bed, carrying the same expression.

Anna was torn between disgust and fascination. Was this down here so the children couldn't see? Was it a kind of art gallery? A morbid, awful gallery?

As she got to the end of the corridor, there was an opening in the floor. A square, black void.

Before she could think any further—

Clank.

A sound.

Clank.

A sound that came from down below.

Clank.

Kneeling at the edge of the hole, Anna shone her flashlight inside: it was a second basement level, but one with a movable ladder to get down, not stairs.

"Hello?" she called out. Praying no one would reply.

Clank.

Grabbing one of the rungs of the ladder, she pulled down on it, causing the mechanism to whirr loudly as it descended into the opening.

The sound of its feet hitting the concrete floor below was loud, and she could tell that the drop wasn't more than a few meters.

Clank.

She stopped for a moment. Was she really going to do this? Go down into the darkness alone? But when she remembered all the death in the house above, this exploration was far less terrifying.

Clank.

Taking a deep breath, she cautiously descended the ladder.

One careful step after another, she reached the cold floor.

This time, there was no light switch on the wall

that she could see. However, there was a bulb on the ceiling.

Clank.

She only had her flashlight to pierce the darkness of what looked like a single large room. Naturally, there were no windows this far underground, and the metal walls showed nothing but a series of equidistant rivets.

Her beam found something else. In the middle of the room, there was a large metal chair. A chair with a metal cuff on the armrests and one on each of the front legs. On the seat itself was a series of large holes, where a bucket sat beneath.

Immediately, the smell of human waste and copper hit her nostrils, and she backed away.

Clank.

"Is anyone there?" she said quietly, getting more nervous, holding her breath from the smell.

Immediately, the *clanks* stopped.

She swept the flashlight across the floor and noticed large rings were fixed onto two metal plates. Ones where a chain had been looped and led off into the darkness at the far side of the room.

Anna needed to leave; this place held nothing except a strange feeling of misery. She was ready to go.

The chains on the floor started to tremble as they were pulled by something.

Clank.

That sound she heard were these chains being

pulled. Pulled by something in the light's recess, out of the range of her flashlight's beam.

She slowly moved back to the ladder, regretting her decision, but before she could reach it, the darkness breached.

Staggering toward her, manacled around the wrists, was a woman. Emaciated, naked, with a body mutilated with horror. Every inch of her skin had gaping wounds, marks, and bruises.

Her thinness was equally as shocking. Her body seemed to lack any muscular definition and appeared like a skeleton draped in broken leather.

On the top of her head was a shiny object. A thick strip of curved metal that covered her eyes like a visor, wrapped around her head, blocking out all sight.

Anna was unable to move.

With a wail, the woman threw her head back and moaned.

As she did, Anna's flashlight caught the inside of the woman's mouth, exposing what was missing: her tongue.

Despite being blinded by the metal, the woman knew that she was not alone. With her chained arms outstretched, she hobbled nearer to Anna, making painful sounds.

Anna turned to climb. But the woman was moving fast, looming in her approach.

As she put one of her feet on the first rung, ready to escape, she heard a sudden crash behind her.

Whirling, she turned her light around and saw

what had happened. The terrifying woman had been pulled down to the ground as she ran out of chain, pulled back by the opposing force of the large metal rings she was tied to.

From the floor, the woman still stretched out her arms, moaning. A painful begging. Like an animal too wounded to attack, the sounds it made turned to whines, then to desperate whimpers.

Anna's mind raced with more realization than confusion as she stared at this tortured woman. Lucie's words were playing in her ears. *They tortured me, Anna... It was them.*

Thinking of the family above and this horror down here, Anna could not begin to fathom the whys or hows as she stepped off the ladder and slowly walked nearer.

"It's okay, I'm not going to hurt you," Anna said, shining the flashlight over the woman's shackles.

Still keeping her distance, she reached out her hand to the woman, and as their fingers touched, the woman instantly calmed down. She even gave Anna a faint, strange smile of relief.

Anna could hardly believe what she was seeing. Could hardly believe that Lucie was not wrong.

The cuffs had worn down the skin on her wrists, making them red raw.

Anna could not stop thinking that the whole family upstairs had to know about this. It was not a secret that the parents could hide from two almost adult children.

. . .

From the basement, through the open sideboard, the tortured girl's moans could be heard calling out. Their echo spreads up from the second basement, across the first and drifted up into the living room.

There, kneeling beside the couch, Anna had buried her head against Lucie's, weeping.

"Forgive me," she muttered. "Please forgive me. I believe you now... I'm so sorry."

The moans from below turned into a more desperate wail.

Anna looked up and wiped her eyes. Now, when she looked around, it gave her a different feeling. No longer one of tragedy, but she felt like justice had been served. Absolute, brutal, unforgiving, but still justice.

She got to her feet and walked out into the kitchen, needing to look once more at Gabrielle. Despite the lack of any facial features, Anna felt she needed to stare at what had become of that woman. That this was a woman who was primarily responsible, just as Lucie said.

Feeling a wave of resentment and hatred rise from within her, Anna raised her fist, ready to strike the corpse, but she held back at the last moment. Not through any moral protest, but because the wails from below were sounding increasingly more pained.

Grabbing the toolbox, the reason she had come up here, she turned, ready to climb back down.

.   .   .

When she got back down to the bottom room, Anna's flashlight immediately caught sight of the captive woman, now curled up by the chair. Making her loud, plaintive groan.

"Hey," Anna said calmly, as she slowly approached, toolbox in hand.

Hearing her voice, the woman fell silent and looked up in her direction. Her hand reached out and grabbed hold of Anna's leg.

Anna stiffened at her cold grasp as it climbed up her, anxiously clinging onto her savior.

Grabbing the screwdriver from the toolbox, Anna turned her attention to the chains.

As the clock struck midday, footsteps could be heard coming up from the upper basement. Slow, agony-filled steps.

Past the grotesque photo gallery, Anna had the mutilated woman propped up, leading her out from the ladder and toward the steps. The woman's feet barely had the strength to hold up her battered frame on her own.

Anna couldn't tell this woman's age, but from her dark, lank hair, the smooth skin between her wounds, she could hazard a guess that she was maybe her age, perhaps a bit older.

Up the staircase to the house, Anna slowly guided the woman. Each step they took left streaks of blood on the metal below. The scabbed lacerations on the woman's soles now reopening from the pressure of walking so far.

She moaned again as her head lolled around. The weight of the metal device over her eyes was weighing down her skull as she tried to understand what was happening.

"Careful," Anna said.

From the sideboard, a long, trembling skeletal hand emerged as the woman blindly walked out. Anna was behind, guiding her out, holding her by her hips.

As the girl's injured bare feet touched the soft carpet of the living room, she let out a shocked sound. Not a pained one, but a confused one.

It was a sensation she couldn't place. Softness beneath her lacerated soles. Not cold concrete. A feeling of comfort she had long forgotten.

As she stepped further onto the carpet, she instantly felt the cool breeze from the night coming in through the smashed living room window. Despite the metal mask covering her eyes, her skin felt the fresh air. The difference stark from the dank staleness below.

From her posture, it was clear that all of this was overwhelming for her. A feeling that was filled with both surprise and trepidation.

As Anna stood behind her, the sight of this woman was made the more horrifying as the living room light revealed more of her body's ruined state. It also illuminated how filthy she really was. Her skin was almost gray with old grime.

Her back was the most terrifying.

Though most of the skin had been flayed long ago, and parts of the woman's spine were on full display between its scar tissue. It was the coil of barbed wire dug into her back that made Anna gasp.

The light also made the object on her head more visible. It was not just a mask, but a cruel device. It blocked out all sight, but the metal straps that held it in place were not only fastened around the back, but held in place with galvanized U nails, embedded through holes in the metal and into the woman's skull.

The woman stood, breathing heavily, unable to coordinate her movements or her balance on this soft surface.

Grabbing the first aid kit from the upstairs bedroom, Anna quickly returned to find the woman crouched in a corner, the cold wall on her back. Its solidity gave this abused woman some familiar calm, something that the warmth and softness did not.

"You're safe now," Anna said.

The woman didn't answer, just sat there huddled.

Taking the antiseptic from the kit, she looked at the third of a bottle that was left swilling at the bottom. It sure wasn't enough, but it was a start.

"Fuck, how is this real?" she mumbled to herself, taking out a handful of gauze pads and looking to clean the freshest of the injuries.

"Can you turn around?" she asked the woman, as she knelt beside her.

Like an obedient child, the woman nodded and turned around.

The barbed wire had to come out first. It looked new, and the injury was far from healed. The skin below was starting to go yellow and leak pus.

With caution, Anna gently took a grip of one of the barbs and pulled on it.

With a high-pitched groan, blood dripped out as the barbs left the woman's skin.

One barb followed another. The woman endured the pain as if it were nothing, staying still as Anna managed to remove the entire coil.

When they were out and the rest of the antiseptic ointment had been applied, Anna realized that there was little she could do to stop any of her infections without medication.

Grabbing a throw from the couch, she gently wrapped it around the woman's shoulders. The woman was now drenched with sweat, her breathing stilted and shallow. When Anna laid her palm against her forehead, she felt it. Her skin was burning up.

In the en-suite bathroom, the woman was lying in the tub, looking blindly anxious. Letting all of this happen, but too scared and confused to do much of anything else.

As the cold water ran from the faucet, touching her feet, she let out a worried yelp.

"Don't be afraid. It's just water."

But the girl started to struggle, kicking out as the tub began to fill, splashing it over the side.

"Shhh! Don't," Anna pleaded. "I'm trying to help you. I need to bring your temperature down."

Gradually, the woman calmed down. She shivered as the water got deeper around her waist.

Anna scooped up a handful of the water and poured some on the lower part of the woman's face, moistening her cracked lips and sallow cheeks. She let out a small, pleasurable yelp as she felt it.

Anna looked at the top of the mask. It was so tight that it had become partially embedded in the woman's flesh. With the large staple-like fasteners embedded in her skull, looking like they had been there for years.

As the cold water rose to her chest. Her temperature started to come down, and she shivered happily. The cold of the basement, being the state she was used to, now calmed her after the initial shock.

Turning off the faucet, Anna put a hand on the woman's shoulder.

"You can understand me, can't you?" she asked.

Turning to her direction, the woman didn't answer.

"Can you?" Anna repeated. "I just want to help."

Hesitantly, the woman nodded.

"I'm going to try and take that thing off your head, is that okay?"

The woman tilted her head in response to the question.

"It might hurt, but I have to try."

As the woman lay in the cold bathwater, Anna took

the screwdriver and moved around to the back of the bath.

"I'm sorry," she said. "It will be quick, okay?"

The woman moaned as Anna slid the screwdriver's tip under the first of the staples.

Taking a breath, she lifted the screwdriver, using it as a lever, against the metal. The woman screamed in agony as the staple lifted out of her head, but she didn't move or fight Anna off.

The staple came out with a wet pop, as a trickle of blood ran out from the hole.

Anna moved the screwdriver's tip under the next staple.

There were at least twenty more.

The whole house reverberated with the screams of the woman as each of the staples was removed.

And with each one, the woman didn't fight back. Didn't move. She just lay obediently in the freezing water, gripping the edge of the bathtub tightly. Unable to hold in the screams.

"I think I got it," Anna said as her fingertips slid under the edges of the mask.

With all the staples removed, the metal contraption was only held by being stuck to her skin.

"Are you ready?" she asked.

Even before she started to lift, the woman started moaning loudly, worried.

The sound that followed was stomach-churning. Matched only in its horror by the piercing of the woman's shrieks.

Underneath the metal, the flesh around her eyes had rotted, so as the metal pulled away, it took away chunks of skin and flesh that had attached to its underside.

Yellow infected gloop ran down her cheeks as the woman was in unspeakable suffering.

Anna was only halfway through and had to pull the rest of the mask hard to free it entirely from the woman's head. As it came away, the straps also took strips of rotting skin with it.

The woman's hands shot up, shielding her eyes. Her very pale, almost luminous blue eyes.

Anna realized what was happening and ran over to the light switch, flicking it off. The glare of the bulb was hurting her eyes, which she had not seen for a while.

In the glow coming in from the hallway, Anna could see that the mask had left a terrible imprint on the woman's skull. The skin underneath that hadn't ripped away was darkened and parchment-like, contrasting with her pale jaw.

. . .

It was late, and none of the neighbors seemed to be any the wiser about what had happened in this house. No one had heard the screams, the gunshots, or seen the bodies lying in the backyard.

Anna had made a decision. She would leave this place before morning. She would leave everything as it was: the open grave, the bodies, the open basement. She would only take Lucie with her to bury far away, and take the woman to a city hospital, leaving her with people who could really help. Then she would disappear, leaving all of this behind her.

With all the lights in the house switched off, the woman no longer screamed. The agony she was in was indescribable, but it was no more than she was used to.

She sat at the foot of the couch, her pale gaze far away.

Anna was there too, ready to move Lucie's body to the car.

"See how peaceful she looks?" Anna said, more to herself than anyone else.

The woman didn't even hear as she continued staring into the dark corner of the room.

"She's s—sleeping like an angel," Anna continued, stammering as her emotion swelled. "It's the first time I've seen her peaceful." She stopped, as the words caught in her throat. "I love you, Lucie."

Overcome with emotion, she lay down beside Lucie's body and held her tight.

She didn't realize how tired she was, as she had fallen asleep within a minute.

. . .

The night carried on, and a horrendous scream woke Anna with a start.

Shocked, she sat up and looked around the shadowy living room.

The woman was no longer there by the couch.

Another scream sounded. It came from the dining room.

Scrambling to her feet, Anna rushed through the doorway.

The screams were coming from behind the other side of the large dining table.

There, the woman screamed in agony as she was mutilating her arm with a kitchen knife and digging its blade deep into her bicep.

Horrified, Anna ran at her, reaching to grab the weapon away.

But the woman fought back.

Her psychotic hysteria multiplied her strength, and she pushed Anna back with ease and immediately started cutting into herself again. But it wasn't just self-abuse; she appeared as if she was cutting into herself to look for something. Something that was under her skin.

Suddenly, her body jerked violently as she collapsed to her side, the knife striking a nerve. As she did, her fingers kept clawing at her new wounds, reaching inside, exploring the flesh. Each movement causing even more shrieking.

She twisted and contorted as she slashed the blade

over more of her skin, then jammed her fingers deep into the wounds.

It was so convincing that Anna instinctively looked at her to see what the woman was trying to get out of her body, but there was nothing. She was just digging into her flesh.

"Please, stop!" Anna yelled to her.

The woman didn't listen as she got to her feet and barged by her, out of the room, slashing and stabbing her own flesh along the way.

She ran back into the living room, back to the corner of the room that felt coldly at home. As she got there, she started slamming her face into the plaster so hard that within seconds, her face was barely more than an open, bloody mess.

Anna ran in after her, trying once again to grab her, to stop her from hurting herself. The whole similarity to the mania that had gripped Lucie was undeniable.

But completely out of control, the woman swiped her bony arm at Anna, smacking her across the cheek and sending her to the floor.

The woman screamed again. A defiant roar filled with torment, as her fingers dug into her wounds, increasingly more frantic. Searching for something only in her mind.

Anna crawled away, realizing that this woman was beyond any help she could offer.

The woman looked down at her, and her eyes

looked petrified. Holding up the knife, she was about to cut into herself again, when—

BANG!

The shot came through the broken window, and in an instant, the woman's head exploded. Demolished it in an instant from her now gushing neck. Her twitching body fell against the wall with a thud.

CHAPTER SEVEN
THE EYES

Before Anna could even think of screaming, two heavily armed men walked from the porch, in through the broken window of the living room.

The first one, a massive figure, held a still-smoking sawed-off shotgun.

Anna was frozen with fear as he saw her and crouched down, the gun resting on his shoulder.

He motioned toward Lucie's body with a nod.

"Who's that then?" he asked, casually.

Anna could not find the words to answer.

The man's smile fell, as he leaned closer.

"I said, *who... is... that?*"

"L–Lucie," Anna managed to gasp.

"Lucie, eh? Lucie, who?" his gaze was unblinking and carried a wealth of threat.

"Lucie... Jurin..."

He nodded. "And you are?"

Anna looked at the man, then at the second,

smaller man, who stood by the window. *Were they the police?* She thought.

"Anna Assaoui," she said nervously. "My name is Anna Assaoui. I just came here. I don't know—"

"Shhh shhh shhh," the man interrupted, shaking his head, before turning to his friend and nodding.

Within seconds, three more men stepped inside, and all four spread through the house.

One checked this room, another two headed upstairs, and the fourth was in the kitchen.

The big man in front of Anna turned back to meet her gaze. "We've been trying to reach the Belfonds for hours. Why couldn't we get through? Can you tell me that?"

Anna stared at him blankly, not having any idea of what he was talking about.

"We tried and tried, but the line was busy," he said. "That doesn't just happen. Not with the Belfonds. That line is to be kept open at all times, for us to call. That's what it's for."

"Hey, Miles," the other man interrupted, holding up the fallen telephone. "It wasn't hung up."

"Ah, that'd do it," the man nodded, not breaking his stare at Anna. "So, are you gonna tell me what the hell's going on?" he asked.

Anna remained silent. Not out of any stubbornness or fear, but because she had no actual clue what was happening.

With a grunt, he reached out and grabbed her by the hair. She screamed as he yanked her to him.

"What the fuck are you doing here, huh?" he grunted. "Tell me now!"

Anna started panicking, trying to drag herself out of his huge hands, but it was a losing battle. She couldn't fight against this goliath's strength.

With a firm grip on her hair, he pulled her to her feet as the other man handcuffed her hands behind her back. She tried to pull herself out of the hold, but couldn't. She was being hauled up the stairs, still by her hair.

"It wasn't me," she screamed. "I didn't kill them!"

She tried to keep her balance, to keep her footing, to match the pace of the man's stride, but her exhaustion didn't allow it. As they got to the top step, her legs buckled below her, and her knees slammed down, scraping along the floorboards, as she was dragged.

Nothing she said or did could slow or change what happened.

He yanked her along as if she weighed nothing, down the hallway to a door on the far left. A door she had not been in—the door to the attic.

On her face was as much fear as disbelief that any of this was actually happening.

Thrown into a dark corner of the attic, she collapsed face-first onto the rough floorboards, unable to brace herself against the impact. Her hands were still locked behind her.

. . .

The house below soon became a lot noisier, as the men bustled about, going room to room, inspecting and clearing up the mess. The bedrooms were tidied, the smashed glass cleaned up, the bodies and bloodstains wiped clean, the sideboard lid repaired and replaced. All as if none of it had ever happened. By the time the clock struck 5 a.m., everything was back to normal, except for some windows missing their panes.

It was methodical, professional, and exact.

They had obviously done this many times within many houses.

Cleaned up and left no trace of the horrors that occurred in them.

Anna had managed to get to her feet and make her way over to the small, round attic window, staring out the back of the house, down to the lawn.

There, one man had picked up Marie's body and walked it down to the open grave. He dropped her in without even a pause. It was as if he were throwing away the weekly trash.

The other two men carried the heavier, ruined remains of Gabrielle. One holding her feet, the other her shoulders. They walked down to the end of the lawn and threw her on top of her family.

Finally, it was Lucie's body that was brought out. Slung over the big man's shoulder, still wrapped in a shroud, looking more fragile and tinier than ever.

As her body was cast onto the Belfond family, Anna broke down.

She bawled, thinking that Lucie, her best and only friend—her love—was now doomed to spend her death in the same pit as the people who ruined her. A hellish punishment, for which Anna prayed that there was no afterlife, that it was just nothing that waited. That there was no more that Lucie would feel or know. Anything aside from that was just unbearable for her to imagine.

In the back yard, the men then filled the hole with large shovelfuls of dirt.

In no time at all, there was no evidence left of the murders that happened here.

The attic was a large space with windows on each side of the house. There was nothing stored or built here. It was just the floorboards, the exposed beams above, and a mass of old cobwebs.

Anna was distraught. She wondered if this was indeed the police, then why was she not in a car being taken to the station for questioning? Why were they burying the bodies?

She then remembered the gunshot and the woman's head being obliterated. If these men were all part of whatever the Belfonds were doing, why would they kill that woman just like that?

Before she could dwell more, a noise from the

opposite window drew her attention. The noise of a car crunching onto the gravel drive.

With her hands aching from being cuffed, and her body from being battered around. She made her way to the window to see.

Behind her own car, a black limousine had pulled up. Even in the dark, with blackened windows and an immaculate shine, it stood out in the surrounding suburbia.

With its engine switched off, the driver's side door opened, and a chauffeur stepped out. Wearing a suit and a hat, he looked as immaculate as the vehicle was.

The armed men were out there too, and rolled a clear tarp all the way from the porch to the passenger side of the car.

The chauffeur opened the door and stood to attention.

Slowly, a female figure appeared. Dressed all in white, she stood on the tarp and nodded at the driver. She was much older, though under the large glasses and the scarf wrapped around her head, little else could be seen.

Walking over, the large man who dragged her here walked out to greet her. Extending a deferential hand to help her along, she instantly refused as she made her own way into the house.

Walking into the living room, the woman looked around, surveying the clean-up work that had been done. The sideboard looked new. The splintered lid now back together, with the photos on top in mended frames, hiding the hammer's holes.

"Ma'am," the big man said from behind. "The rugs should be washed within the hour, and the replacement windows are en route."

With a wrinkled smile, she nodded. "Efficient as ever, Miles," she said, turning to him. "Is there anything you can't do?"

"Nope," he replied, returning her smile, and motioning to the stairs. "We put her in the attic," he added.

Anna could hear the footsteps on the stairs as the light above her was switched on. She winced at the light after her time in the shadows.

Nervous, she moved back against the wall, into the shadows that the light didn't fully touch.

At the door, the key clacked as it opened the lock.

Miles appeared first. He looked around the room to make sure she was still cuffed, then turned and nodded behind him.

"Mademoiselle," he said.

That was the only name he knew to call the old woman, and the only name she answered to. She walked over, unhurried, staring into the shadows where Anna now hid. Her heels clacked loudly on the floor.

A second man followed inside, carrying a chair. He

walked to where Mademoiselle now stood and placed it down for her.

She nodded to him, and he walked back to stand next to Miles by the door.

Mademoiselle sat in the chair under the attic's lightbulb. With her perfect posture and luxurious clothing, she seemed quite aristocratic. She slowly removed her headscarf, revealing white hair that was perfectly pulled back, her rosy makeup, and dark maroon lipstick, which accentuated her elegant appearance. Yet age had clearly left its mark on someone who was obviously once a radiant beauty. She was no younger than seventy-five, and her face carried a wealth of deep wrinkles.

As she spoke, her voice was hoarse from years of cigarettes, yet still refined. Every syllable was pronounced and exact.

"Lucie Jurin escaped us fifteen years ago, did she not?" she asked, with a polite tone.

From the shadows, Anna stared out, lost.

"Did she not?" Mademoiselle repeated, staring at her through her thick-framed glasses.

Her voice was calm, yet it carried a terrifying authority that made Anna nod quickly.

The old woman smiled knowingly. "Yes, good. I am glad we have that squared away... That one was such a pity. But she got away, so all that work on her was for naught. I must say that I kept an eye on her for a while. However, we had to move on and find the next subject. It seems, though, that she did not move on. Not at all."

She took off her glasses and folded them. Handing them out, the other guard quickly stepped forward and took them from her, like an armed butler at her service.

She continued. "You see, that was at a time when we were... let us say... a little bit less organized. Almost clumsy in what we did compared to today. Now, don't get me wrong, we still got results, but it was not as careful as it should have been." She chuckled to herself as she shook her head. "To think we used that disgusting slaughterhouse... What were we thinking?"

She leaned forward in her chair toward Anna, smiling. "It is almost poetic is it not? That Gabrielle let her slip away all those years ago, and then, after fifteen years, she was found? That kind of revenge has a certain flair to it, does it not? I could not dream of blaming that girl for doing what she did.... She was a victim after all. Like all the others." She stopped as her mood darkened. "But it is easy to create a victim, my dear...So easy."

For a moment, she appeared lost in thought. "You lock a living thing in the dark, away from the daylight... and they begin to suffer. Then you feed that suffering. Methodically, systematically, coldly. Building it up more each day. And you keep it constant. A break in the constant undoes all work. All hope must die."

She carried on solemnly, her emotions detached. "The subject will go through many states. And after a while, the trauma... A tiny crack in the mind that is so easy to create.... Allows them to see things that have no existence."

She paused, savouring the anticipation.

"What did she see, your poor Lucie? From what I understand she had quite the torment. Her doctor's reports were very colorful."

Anna was stunned and shocked by the question.

"Was it reliving the horror, seeing it around all corners? Or was it monsters? Or people coming after her to take her back... We have seen it all, trust me."

Anna still stared, unable to believe.

Her reaction cracked a cynical smile on Mademoiselle's face. "Things that wanted to hurt her, for sure, yes? That is always the common thread. They just take a myriad of forms. So, which is it, and please stop with the silence; I don't want to force it out of you. That is so boring. Torture should not be for anything aside for the greatest of truths."

Anna slowly lowered her head and spoke in a fearful tone. "It was a dead woman... she told me she saw a dead woman."

The woman laughed in triumph. "There! A dead woman! That is perfect, is it not? She hadn't suffered for very long at all, and she saw a dead woman? What was it?" she turned to Miles for an answer. "A year or so?"

He nodded to her.

"That's child's play... But I guess, she *was* a child back then."

She then spoke as if confiding. "The woman you found down there... Sarah Dutreuil... She saw insects. Cockroaches, beetles, everywhere, running under her skin ... She would have cut off her own arm rather than endure them. And we encouraged that mania. Pity it ended up as it did, but you broke the routine. You let in hope. Four years of work, gone. Poof. Vanished.... But that is all part of life. Part of the rich tapestry we call fate."

She paused, thoughtfully.

"You see, Life... Life out there. It's getting worse. People no longer consider what true suffering is. The world as it is now is such that there are only victims left of invented issues or paltry reasons. There is no real lasting pain left... and martyrs? Martyrs are almost extinct. Very rare."

Her smile returned. "Now, a martyr... that, *that* is something else. Something sacrosanct. Something very, very holy. Something pure and simple yet beyond rational thought."

As she continued, she brought out an old leatherbound folder from her coat pocket.

"A martyr is a truly exceptional human being. They transcend suffering. They transcend the deprivation of all things. They transcend the depths of cruelty... They are burdened with the evils of the earth, and still they surrender, they surrender and transform. They transmogrify. Do you understand that word, my dear? Transmogrify? They transfigure their souls with a divinity that is, in my eyes anyway, quite magical."

Turning the folder to Anna, she showed the embroidered letter on its front. A golden M.

"Garish, I know," she smiled as she opened the cover.

Inside, mounted on red velvet-covered cards, were the same photos that hung in frames in the basement.

She held up the first picture. The same one Anna stared at in horror. The one of the Chinese peasant woman. Her amputated arms, her flayed torso, the indifference of the executioners, the laughing of the crowd. Her eyes staring upward as a strange smile on her face.

"This was taken in Long Sheng Province, 1911 or 1912. We unfortunately do not know her name, but we do know that she did not believe in any God. She refused any prayers to be said to her before they administered her punishment." She paused as she looked at the photo. "Can you guess as to what crime resulted in such barbarism? What she could possibly have done to warrant this level of horror?"

She didn't need or want Anna to answer.

"She tried to steal a chicken... Her family was starving. The farmer nearby had hundreds of chickens. She snuck in at night and stole one, thinking no one would ever know... Well, she paid very dearly for that act." She turned the photo back to Anna, holding it closer to her. "When the photo was taken, the woman was still alive... Now look at her eyes."

Anna saw them. Saw the surreal expression.

The woman turned the next mounted image to her. One that showed a shaven, tortured woman in a village square. Chained to a post. Her naked body beaten, whipped, gouged.

"Jouans-Lussac, 1945. The Liberation. This woman in question ran a grocery store. One that had been part of the village for over a hundred years. She was known and liked by all. Her name was Jeanette Mille. Her crime was that she slept with a German soldier. It didn't matter that he raped her. At the time, the men saw it as a desecration to be punished... she was beaten... then, quite ironically, raped by every Frenchman in the village. One after the other. Some also stabbed her. Some burned her. But all 232 men who lived there partook in the rape. All to teach her a lesson. And every wife of these men witnessed with pride. Their husbands... standing up for France... as it were... Again, in this photo... she was alive. Though barely... Now... *Look at her eyes!*"

Anna did. She saw the same expression. The exact look.

The next image was thrust forward, an emaciated woman on a stained hospital bed.

Anna started to feel weaker and weaker, as the woman's words were beginning to blend together.

"General Hospital of Birmingham, 1960. Helena Bukowiec. Daughter of Polish immigrants. Declared an atheist. Here she was, terminally ill with cancer. Cancer of the lungs, stomach, brain, bones, and pancreas. There were no stages to declare how doomed she was, and the pain she suffered. Not at the hands of others, though, but at the hands of her own body.

Morphine, unfortunately, had no effect on her. She was immune. So she felt it all with extreme clarity... In this photo, she was alive, and minutes from death... *Look at her eyes...*"

The repeated line rang in Anna's ears.

Look at her eyes.

The next photo was shown.

"Samantha Howe. Worthing, England. 1972. She was beaten by her husband. No reason, just a drunken, cruel man who beat her mercilessly and locked her in the house. He broke her bones by throwing her downstairs and hitting her with a cricket bat. And all her injuries had to set naturally. In the end, her body was a contorted and shattered mess. Her breaks set incorrectly you see? And the infections from her wounds never saw a moment of care... This was where they found her at the bottom of the cellar. She hadn't eaten in a week. Hadn't moved in days, not by choice. She couldn't. Her broken bones would no longer carry her... She just existed there in terrible pain. She was alive in this photograph that the police took when they were tipped off by a neighbour... Now... *Look at her eyes.*"

And the next.

"This one, Birta Hansdottir. Reykholt, Iceland. 1982. Spent nine hours trapped in a car wreck, the engine having ripped through the lower half of her body. The heat of the metal seared the wounds closed, so she bled to death quite slowly, and in indescribable pain. Eventually, the firefighters arrived five minutes before she passed away. Now... *Look at her eyes.*"

Just like all of them, the eyes and strange smiles were the same. Like they all looked at the same thing with the same emotion.

The leather folder closed, and Mademoiselle held it close to her chest as she carried on.

"All of them were the same, my dear! Do you comprehend what I'm saying? They were all alive when their photos were taken. They were from all over the world. From different cultures and beliefs. And to think, people still believe that the concept of martyrdom is a religious invention."

She slid the folder back in her pocket.

"They try to tell you a martyr is a person who suffered because of their beliefs. This is proven to be an outright lie told by zealots. A martyr is someone who transcends because of the suffering. They need no God to see beyond the veil... To see this meaning. I personally do not believe any martyrdom can be achieved by the faithful. I do not see how you can be a martyr if you are conditioned to believe. For instance, Catholic testimonies from their so-called martyrdoms are pathetic. They speak of angels, golden arches, and little clouds. Holy nonsense, the lot of it! They see what they have been taught to see. There is no truth in their suffering. It is just their brain repeating the lies in their dying moments. They show no real truths, and you can see that in their eyes."

She lowered her voice.

"But, my dear, transmogrified souls have very much existed, and they see the *real* truth."

Mademoiselle turned and signaled the men with a wave of her hand. She then looked back at Anna coldly.

"All suffering must be graded. Handled and administered with care and thought. Otherwise, the subject will block what is being offered; their trauma becomes numb. You see, we have tried everything, even children. Like your friend... But always, *always*, it is women who attain true martyrdom. Males cannot. They cannot process the pain in the same way. Women are the masters of agony. Always have been... and I swear to you, that's the truth. Don't ask me how or why."

As the men got closer, Anna grew even more worried as she saw the metal bar that Miles held in his hand.

"Why are you telling me all this?" Anna whimpered, pleadingly from the shadow.

"Why?" The old woman laughed heartily. "You really don't realize?"

The next thing Anna knew, the man was rushing forward, a metal bar held up in attack.

The next time she woke, Anna's head rang with an intense ache.

Her cheeks were cold from lying on the damp and stagnant concrete floor. As she blearily opened her eyes, she could see nothing in the pitch black. The smell in here was distinct and one she had experienced only hours before. Blood mixed with human waste.

Anna hadn't realised that blood even had a smell until today. But when the metallic tang hit her nose, it sickened her even more than the smell of the excrement.

As her weariness abated and she realized the reality of where she was, as she felt the metal cuffs around her ankles and wrists, she let out a terrible scream.

CHAPTER EIGHT
RITUAL

The lights in the room blasted on with a brilliance that stung Anna's eyes. She had been left down in the lower basement in only underwear and a small t-shirt. Neither of which were hers, and neither were her size, and neither did anything to stop the cold of the metal and concrete room from making her whole body shiver.

Miles had come down to the lower basement and dragged Anna kicking and screaming to the metal chair in the middle of the room. She had fought him as hard as she could. She tried to punch, kick, bite, and headbutt, but Miles' huge hands made all her efforts futile.

But Miles did nothing more. He didn't even look at her as the second cuff clicked, locking her in place. He just nodded to himself, satisfied with a job completed, turned, and climbed up the ladder out of there.

Now, cuffed to the chair with the perforated seat, with the plain metal walls around her, she waited for what would come next. Under her, the bucket sat, still carrying the remnants of the woman's time here.

The light was then turned off, and she was cast once more into total blackness.

Time passed. She didn't know how long. She could not guess if it were minutes or hours.

But with each ticking second, Anna didn't get more upset. She got more rageful. She became enraged with a fury that came out in screaming into the darkness.

'Let me go' became 'Please, I won't tell anyone' became 'I'll fucking kill you all, every last one of you.'

Her pride refused this situation. Refused to accept that this was happening. Refused to allow herself to succumb to it.

But in the dark, damp chill, her screams and yells of anger soon fell to a horrified whine.

Her head lolled back and forth as her exhaustion played havoc. Her legs twitched, her mouth let out moans she didn't know she was making. She hadn't even known that she had wet herself into the bucket until she heard a liquid sound hitting the slop in the bucket below and realized it was from her.

The rage evaporated as the fear took a hard and unrelenting grip. She remembered that awful woman she had found down here. With her metal mask and the sores and wounds covering her body. Then Lucie... what she went through.

. . .

She had passed out countless times, but had no way of knowing how long for. Each time she came to, she felt even more disconnected, until all her senses started to blur. She even stopped being able to smell the bucket. She just felt the pain in her body. The metal of the chair, the damp floor beneath her bare feet. The sting of the cold on her skin. The numbness that came and went. One moment, she felt nothing, then the next, her nerves all screamed at her. It was like a rollercoaster of torment that came at her in relentless waves.

By the time the light was switched back on, and the room was filled with a brightness that stung her eyes, she had changed from the person who had been brought down here.

Gone was any trace of strength. She couldn't even find the strength to close her eyes, to protect herself from the glare; she just sat there, accepting the discomfort.

She was slumped in the chair, her underwear stained yellow and brown, with the contents of her bowels trapped in her panties, unable to fall through the holes in the chair, mashed against her skin.

The black circles under her eyes had deepened, and her mouth hung ajar. Her lips were dry and cracked, and she was zoning in and out of consciousness and passing out for a few seconds at a time, before coming to again.

One moment she was on her own in the dark, the next time the light was on, and someone was there, tapping a finger on her cheek. No words, just action.

She struggled to come to, struggled to wake from her haze.

The slap then came. Hard across the cheek, forcing her senses to wake as she yelped in shock and pain.

Before she could even turn back, a bowl filled with a dubious concoction of mush was held in front of her. A woman she did not recognize stood before her with a blank expression. She did not wait for Anna to fully escape the lethargy that consumed her, as a spoonful of the rancid food was shoveled into her mouth.

As the foulness was forced in, she gagged. Coughing from the large spoon reaching the back of her mouth, but also the grim taste of decay that suddenly washed over her taste buds.

She couldn't help it, but she instinctively spat the matter back out. And as she did, her face was met with another hard slap.

The spoon was refilled and another helping forced.

Even when she wailed in torment, it did nothing. Each time she didn't swallow, another slap followed by an immediate spoonful. When she eventually managed to swallow, it made her stomach retch so hard that it brought the food back up involuntarily. But that didn't stop what was happening. Whatever she spat or vomited back was spooned right back in.

And nothing stopped until the bowl was empty, and she was left covered in the spat-up remnants.

· · ·

Her consciousness drifted, saving her from the reality of where she was, but her brain was so beaten that no dreams waited for her. No images of things past. No comfort. It was just darkness. And when she was awake, it was nightmarish enough.

She had woken with her head tilted back, staring into the nothingness above. But it was so black that she had no idea if her eyes were open or closed.

The lights burst on again.

The ladder came down again.

The woman came down again.

The bowl in her hand again.

Another serving of muck was forced down her throat.

The next time this happened, she fought a little bit less.

The next time this happened, she fought even less.

By the tenth time this happened to her, she didn't fight at all and gave in to the abuse. It became a ritual where she opened her mouth to weakly accept the offering. Without any protest, she chewed what she needed to before swallowing. Her stomach was too ruined to fight against what she was given.

Her eyes, though, had stopped looking at the woman. Now they just stared at nothing. Focused ahead without any comprehension.

The spaces between the feedings were vacuous.

Her only companion there in the dark was the sound of her own wheezes and moans.

When she slept, it was only for a short amount of time, as her body woke her up with a new soreness. She couldn't stand, walk around, or even move as she was locked in the chair. She was stuck on that hard surface.

And as she ate, her digestion still worked, but what was expelled from her became less and less solid, to the point it fell out through the fabric of her underwear like rusty water.

When she tried to speak, it was a wheeze of words that escaped her lungs.

"Lucie."

She had no idea, but she now repeated that name, so quietly that it was barely a sound. It came with each exhalation she made. Over and over, as hours bled into days.

She remained, repeating. But then all coherence disappeared, and what came out was just a moan.

. . .

Was it the nineteenth or twentieth feeding? She didn't know, but the food was followed by something else. The woman stood behind her with a large pair of scissors, clumsily cutting her hair close to the scalp.

Anna had no strength to stop it, but felt every part of its intention. With her hair unevenly removed, it was a humiliation. A stripping of identity. It was not necessary.

The whole way through the process, her teeth chattered, and had done so for as long as she could remember being. That was now just what they did. Not from cold or stress, though that is what started them, but now her body was fighting something else. The blow she had taken from the hammer had broken the skin, and as she had not received any medical attention, the wound was yellow, and her body was struggling.

What hair had been cut, lay over and around her. Not a strand being cleared up.

She left only to return soon after, a glass of water in her hand.

Anna heard the clink and fizz of a tablet being dropped into it, before her chin was yanked up and the whole measure poured down her throat in one.

What did the sun feel like? She thought to herself. *What did warmth feel like?* She had no memory of it.

The solitude and hurt of this room encompassed her to such a degree that the time before started to feel unreal. Lucie felt unreal. Her mother felt unreal. Whose whole life felt like a fever dream... and now in this hellish pit, that was the real, true reality.

She tried to remember, but as she clung to a thought, an image, her brain darkened. Shifted. And she blacked out.

She didn't know the day, date, or even the month.

Time was not part of her world here. It was just an existence of cyclical misery. When the tears had dried and the screams all voiced, all that was there was her... in the darkness.

13 MONTHS LATER

Existence had become a wretched purgatory, as Anna was still in the second basement of what was the Belfond house.

With the repeated harrowing met upon her, the extreme nature of her captivity only increased the longer she was here.

It was during this month that, with each meal, a new ritual began.

At first, it was a slap.

A slap became a punch.

A punch became two punches.

Until mealtime brought with it a full beating. All at the hands of the woman.

. . .

Outside, the summer sun shone on the suburban streets. Children played on their bikes as parents mowed the lawns. Idyllic living akin to a Norman Rockwell painting that betrayed the real decade and, aside from the cars parked here, could have easily been in 1950s America.

Underneath number six, though, in its second basement, was something akin to the Spanish Inquisition, but without a God and without any demand for answers.

Today, Anna was unclasped from the chair and thrown into a corner of the room, her back smacking into the riveted metal wall. She fell like a wet cloth, her t-shirt and underwear the same as the day she was cast down here, but now almost black with filth. Her hair still cut short, and her body covered in scars and bruises.

The woman stood above her, raining down a storm of slaps, punches, and kicks.

Yet the blows didn't push Anna to unconsciousness. It did not weaken her anymore. She was as weak as she possibly could be. Each impact that came was horrifically paradoxical as each woke her up a bit more. Each gave her a jolt of energy that stopped her from passing out. It was not a matter of her will, but rather her body's survival instinct.

Each hit took her back to her childhood. To the beatings she received back then. To the horrible abuse she had to make herself detach from. The pain she had to ignore so that she could live. The same thing she did here without even realizing.

The pain existed and battered her flesh, bruised her muscles, cracked her bones, but she could not let herself feel it. She could not give in.

This was all she had.

As the boots came down, slamming into her gut, she had no screams and only made distorted moans as her lungs exhaled. Her hands were weakly held out in a pitiful gesture for the attack to stop, but it was instinct, not intention.

As the fist came down and smacked into her face, she gurgled, and as it did, syllables fell over her bloody lips. Not words. Words had not come for a while.

As this torturer worked without emotion, without hatred, she suddenly stopped. The requisite amount of punishment now dealt.

Stopping, she dragged Anna back to her feet and cuffed her into the chair once more.

The food bowl was then produced, and she was forced to eat the slop through gasps and groans.

When it was finished, she left the room. The ladder brought up behind her.

The next time Anna woke, she came to as her neck was grabbed. She was dragged to her feet and thrown against the metal wall once more, her face colliding with it.

Her already broken nose broke again, and the

wound opened wide. Her already split lip gushed. One of her teeth cracked and fell out onto the floor.

Then she grabbed Anna again.

Smashed her face into the metal again.

With eyes wide and glassy, Anna managed to find her scream once more.

Though it did not stop the assault.

Each time she thought she had grown accustomed to the horror, the horror increased and brought the fear back again.

Another week later, and more punches before her meal.

Her belly was already black with bruises, and the additional violence only made them worse.

Falling to her knees, the beating stopped, and the woman walked around her. Anna's front was done for now. Now she beat on other parts of her, one after the other.

Her back.

Then her legs.

Her arms.

And with each, Anna's screams came, but they were more animal than human.

Until...

16 MONTHS LATER

Anna was no longer Anna.

Her face was swollen, marked, caked in dirt, and disfigured by bruises, so much so that she was unrecognizable from the woman she once was.

In the black, she was no longer confined to the chair. Instead, she was shackled to the chains, sluggishly walking around the small room like a zombie. Her arm rubbed against the cold walls as she went. Her weakened legs threatened to give up with each labored step that she took.

Each breath was a strangled wheeze, where each inhalation hurt and stung in her lungs, and when she swallowed, it felt like choking on sand.

After so long being down, her mind was in a constant fog, but as her steps slowed, a ghost of lucidity swept over her. As it did, she could do nothing but weep.

39 MONTHS LATER

Seated and restrained once more in the metal chair, Anna's face was no longer swollen, but emaciated. She was somehow even less of who she had been.

Her wrists were gnawed and lacerated from the cuff's restraint, and bleeding constantly.

As a sponge soaked in cool water passed over her forehead, she showed no reaction. No relief. This sudden reprieve from the cruelty brought her no comfort.

A glass of water came up to her lips, and she obediently drank it, all while her eyes stared out unfocused.

The care of the sponge and drink was soon replaced as the beating commenced once more.

Buy now, the rhythm of the punches across her body did little.

The dull, meaty slaps were only sounds in this room. All gasps and screams absent.

No complaint. No instinctive sound of pain. Just the sound of the hits and her same unfocused stare.

But she knew what this meant... Worse was coming. She did not know when.

42 MONTHS LATER

Asleep on the damp ground, among her own filth, Anna slept.

Her hair was gone. She was bald, and her head was covered in cuts, having been shaved off with a blunt razor.

A new sound of creaking metal roused her from her sleep.

The darkness in the room broke as an unusual, dull light spilled out, not from the bulb above.

Anna's eyes looked up from the floor and saw that at one end of the room, the wall had rolled back on an unseen mechanism, and in its place was another room.

With little strength, Anna got to her feet, staring into this light.

What she saw didn't belong here. It was a dining room in an old apartment, where she grew up. It was the same, with the same faded wallpaper and the same shelves of books lining the walls.

At the table, a woman sat, a small television on the sideboard casting her silhouette in a weak bluish glow. One that spilled onto Anna's confused face.

As she stepped closer to the surreal vision, she could see the woman in more detail. She was in her fifties and had a very worn and tired face. It was her mother, just as she used to be.

On the table in front of her, the remnants of a dinner remained. Four mostly empty plates of meat and vegetables, alongside empty glasses and bottles of drink.

Anna hobbled in. She stared at her mother, who turned to her with a smile.

"Did you eat?" the woman said. "Sorry, we didn't leave you any."

Anna looked at her, unsure of what to do.

"The cat got your tongue?"

Through her dry sore throat, Anna managed to reply. The first word she had spoken in a long time.

"Mom?"

The woman's face turned to a scowl. "You were *with* her, weren't you?

Anna stared back.

"You *shame* me, and your whole family," her mother shook her head. "You are *perverse!*"

As Anna answered, she was no longer a captive. Standing in her mother's house. Her hair grown. Her clothes clean. Her body unmarked by torture.

"I love her, Mom," she said. "But that's not what you—"

The woman slammed her fist on the dining room table, shaking the crockery.

"It disgusts me!" she shouted. "*You* disgust me! I wish you were dead."

"Mom..." Anna gasped, about to cry.

"And not just me.... Your uncle... we did *everything* for you! You shame me and you shame him." She grimaced and looked away. "You're filth!"

"But he—he did things to me, Mom," Anna cried. "You know what he did!"

"Oh, be quiet," the woman said as she picked up her wine glass and took a gulp.

"Please... believe me."

The mother then hurled her glass across the room. "*SHUT UP!*" she screamed as it collided against a bookshelf and shattered loudly. "You're a *whore!*"

She turned to Anna, but as she did, her face was different. It was now warped. Twisted. Gnarled. As if it had been made of clay then each part reshaped and moved. One eye was too big and higher. The mouth was as wide as her skull. Her nose tilted.

"You *made* him do that to you!" she sneered. "You asked for it. You *wanted* it!"

She shot a look behind Anna.

"Show her, Michel. Show her what she made you do."

Anna didn't want to, but she turned around.

The lower basement was no longer there. Instead, it was her bedroom, just as it had been when she was a child.

Stood by her bed... fat, naked, sweaty, rubbing himself was her uncle. Grinning as he made himself harder and harder.

Slowly, he walked toward her, giggling as his rubs turned to strokes.

Her mother gleefully laughed from behind. "Show this cunt how we should have slaughtered her like a pig when she was born."

Anna, though, was not really there. She was standing in the lower basement, in chains, staring at the metal wall, muttering to herself.

There was no dining room. No bedroom. No mother. No uncle. No horrific memory come to life. Just her mania shattering her.

Anna wailed as she swung her arm in defence as the space in front of her, before backing away to escape the thing that didn't exist.

She lifted her arm to protect her head, then hurled herself with all her weight across the room. Slamming into the metal wall and collapsing in agony to the floor.

She achingly got to her feet, then did it again. Threw herself across the room, and this time she slammed into the chair.

Her screams, her sobs, finally found a voice after months of being lost.

Upstairs, in the living room of the old Belfond house, the television was on. The screen displayed a live feed from the lower basement, captured by a camera discreetly hidden in a corner.

Marta and Pierre Bastion sat on the sofa, watching.

"What do you think she's seeing?" Marta said, intrigued.

Pierre shrugged, finding it all quite amusing. "Who knows. Something she doesn't like anyway. What does it matter?"

"Well, if this continues, we'll have to put the mask on her. Can't have her doing this to herself."

CHAPTER NINE
WITNESS

58 MONTHS LATER

Anna was seated in the lower basement, chained, as the lights shone brightly above her. She was still, breathing shallowly. Her skin, though still dirty, was so pale now that it appeared like porcelain through the blood and filth.

Her body was so skeletal that each rib in her chest could be seen, and her arms and legs were just bone with little muscle on them. Her breasts, once full, were now almost gone. She was too frail to stand, too weak to hold her own weight. Both of her hands had all their fingers missing, cut off without any precision. Only her thumbs remained, with stumps of varying short lengths, each only partially healed.

Her age would be a mystery to anyone who tried to guess. She could have been sixteen or sixty. Male or female. Alive or dead.

From behind her, the metal wall let out a loud click.

Anna didn't move or even appear alerted to this sound, as a door appeared in the wall. A door that had only started to open over the past year. A room where she was dragged into daily, as the beatings were no longer enough. The escalation becoming surgical.

From inside, Pierre Bastion peered out. Wearing a face mask, a hair scarf, and gray hospital scrubs. He looked at her and nodded to the man next to him. Miles.

"You can bring her in now," Pierre said.

Without another word, Miles walked over and knelt beside Anna.

She paid him no attention as her chains were unfastened. Dropping them to the floor, he grabbed her by the back of her neck, then lifted her with ease. She didn't even moan as she hung there. Her arms and legs dangling like a marionette as he carried her into the other room. Her heels dragging along the concrete floor.

When inside, Pierre closed the door, motioning the large man to the far end of the room.

The glow of a gas lamp drenched this terrifying room in a phosphorescent yellow.

Along one side of the room, on a large wall, all perfectly arranged on hooks, were tools of every size and use. Tools that pierced, cut, crushed, and tore. Tools of bluntness and tools of precision.

Along the other side were cages of mice and rats, as well as terrariums swarming with insects.

She was dragged to the metal operating table and laid down upon it, her body strapped down.

Over the past months, she had been wrapped in barbed wire. She had her flesh drilled, burned, and cut. She had needles stabbed into her nerve endings. Sharp things jammed through her skin. She had been suffocated. She had been drowned. Her teeth had been smashed. Her toes and fingers were broken slowly, then deliberately removed. Acid had been poured on her skin. Fire had burned the soles of her feet.

And when all manner of torturous depravity was forced upon her, after a while, she didn't cry or scream.

And she was never alone.

Aside from this doctor and the large guard, someone else was always there. Standing in the corner, watching. Someone who had not left since she saw the wall open.

Her mother and Uncle.

No matter what she endured, they were there watching with malice. No one else saw them, but she could. And she heard their words repeating constantly.

"Whore. Whore. Whore. Whore."

After the latest round of abuse, she was taken back into her room.

Again, to the perforated chair.

The feeding ritual was about to commence.

. . .

The woman held her bowl and spoon and began the feeding.

As ever, she was compliant, as she swallowed the vile mixture without complaint.

As before, days were abstract. There was no sun. No moon. No time.

Her food was given once a day, and it could have been breakfast, lunch, or dinner for all she knew.

It was a calculated and programmed schedule of suffering.

Not separate events, but an existence of continuous and methodical brutality.

"It's time," Pierre said.

"Will she survive it?" Miles asked.

"I don't think so. Do we have another one lined up in case? I think this one's a dud, and we should just move on."

"Yeah, we have a few in holding."

Miles walked in and unlocked her bindings before moving her into the torture room. But unlike before, he did not drag her, and he was not forceful. Instead, he picked her up gently in his arms and walked her in.

He didn't stop at the operating table. The one that she had lain on many times before. Now she was being taken further into the room, where a large metal device stood. Part rack, part turning wheel. It was a frame designed to hold a body still while it could be rotated with a single pull of a lever, exposing every side of its occupant to the surgeon.

He placed her carefully in the rack. Cuffing her wrists, biceps, ankles, and calves in place. He then gently brought down a clamp for her head, which, with the bracing poles. Kept her completely immobile.

Pierre walked over and pulled the lever. When he did, the whole rack turned 180 degrees, so she was now facing down to the floor.

This new sensation made her react again. Her swollen eyes opened wider, in worry about what was about to happen.

Rolling a small metal tray of implements over, Anna could see what they were. Forceps, a pile of gauze sponge, a tub of arterial clamps and a row of various implements—all scalpels. From thin-gauge razors to thicker blades, they all gleamed in the light.

She was held tightly in the rack, and no matter how much she tried, she was unable to stop the first blade from being picked up, as Pierre leaned over her back.

The blade cut into her grime-caked t-shirt, slicing the only clothing she had worn in years. With two long motions, the fabric opened. With little effort, he pulled it from the rack, leaving her topless. Not that there was any shame in her anymore to protest.

Pierre looked at her panties with some disgust. They were crusted with her own waste from over the years. When the scalpel cut into them, they almost cracked off.

Anna's eyes darted from left to right, panicking silently. Confused as to what was happening.

Pierre then picked up a larger scalpel and placed it to Anna's back.

Then it started.

The blade sliced effortlessly into her skin. It was not a deep cut and went through the epidermis and just beyond the subcutaneous layer. The blade was so sharp that it felt like an ice cube was being run across her skin.

When the scalpel had cut three long adjoining lines around her shoulder blade, the scalpel was returned to the tray, dripping with blood. He picked up a large, curved blade.

Her nerves soon shredded as the doctor took the forceps and gripped them into her wound. Pulling up the skin, he used the curved blade to cut the flesh away, allowing him to peel her skin off her like it was an orange.

She went to scream, but no air came out of her lungs. Her cracked mouth was open wide, but she just froze still. The agony she felt was unlike anything that had come before. Beyond all that had been done to her, nothing burned through her like this.

On the floor sat an empty, white plastic container. Pierre leaned over it and dropped her fifteen-inch strip of skin into it. It squelched as it landed, and Anna could only stare at it.

The removal of her skin was done fast and without pause. Pierre performed it methodically and carefully, minimizing all unnecessary trauma. But even so, without any anaesthesia, it wracked her body into paralysis, and sent the blood spilling to the floor.

The pain did not stop as the skin was removed; the exposed patch of flesh continued to burn as if it were happening constantly. The sensation didn't disappear or dull as Pierre picked up a piece of gauze sponge and dabbed it on her wound, mopping up as much of the blood as possible. He then grabbed an arterial clamp to stop the major bleeding from ending this surgery too early.

He moved on to the next patch of skin. The scalpel's cut felt like ice once again, then was followed by another wave of searing pain.

The sheet of wet skin slopped into the white container on top of the first.

Anna's scream was still trapped inside, as slowly, so very slowly, she started to dislocate from her mind.

As another square of skin was removed, and as another arterial clamp stemmed the thick flow of blood, she felt herself falling back, deep into a hole. A safe hole. A painless hole.

In the murky light of this room, Miles witnessed this emotionlessly and didn't flinch once as sheet after sheet was cut from her body.

And when the back was done, Pierre pulled the

lever, and the metal rack spun, moving Anna's body face up.

Her expression had not changed. Wide-eyed, wide-mouthed, stuck in a mental well of shock.

And Pierre then continued.

His gloves, scrubs, and apron were now drenched in red, as he continued his work.

Toeless feet first. Up the legs, to the groin, to the waist, to the chest, the breasts, both arms... until only her head was left with skin.

But he was not finished.

Lastly came the back and sides.

What started at 1:01 p.m. ended at 4:34 p.m., and all that was left, all that remained untouched by the scalpel, was Anna's face.

Her face, stuck in that same expression.

With the arteries all clamped off, Pierre looked at her in surprise.

Clacking the lever once more, the rack whirred, moving Anna upright.

With an impressed shake of his head, he turned and walked away.

"She's quite incredible," he said, passing Miles, who followed closely behind.

Anna remained. Staring. Frozen.

· · ·

In the backyard of the Belfond house, it was late afternoon, and the sun shone its remaining rays of the day upon the lawn.

At the far end, where bodies were once buried, large bushes now grew. All were fed with the nutrients from the decaying below.

From the side of the house came a whirring sound, as a small scooter zipped around the lawn. Maxim Bastion whooped with joy as he sped over the grass. At only seven years old, he knew nothing of what lay in the earth or what dwelled deep under the house.

From the back door, Marta leaned out.

"Maxim, it's getting late, come inside!" she shouted.

"Aw, Mom," the boy complained. "Just a little longer, please!"

"You can play more tomorrow, now come in."

With a shrug, the boy obeyed. Getting off his scooter, he wheeled it to the back door, propping it against the house.

When he got inside, Marta was there. She ran her hand through his hair. "Did you put the scooter away or leave it outside the door again?"

The boy looked guilty. "It's just outside the door."

"Last time, it stayed out in the rain, didn't it? Got all rusty. We can't buy you a new one every year, you know!"

"I'm sorry," he said. "I'll put it in the garage."

"Well, it's not supposed to rain tonight," she

smiled. "So it'll be our secret. Okay? Now go upstairs and brush your teeth."

Maxim smiled and ran into the house.

"Clean them properly, okay?"

"Two minutes," the boy called back from the staircase.

Marta laughed. "Exactly right, two minutes and no less!" she confirmed.

As the boy went upstairs, his father, Pierre, appeared from the living room. Walking out of the basement entrance in the sideboard, he had removed his bloody medical gear and looked exhausted after the long surgery.

He walked into the kitchen and kissed his wife on the cheek.

"She made it?" Marta asked.

Pierre nodded, impressed. "Surprising, right? Never would have guessed it."

"Is Miles still down there?" she asked.

He nodded as he walked through to the downstairs bathroom.

Marta picked up a steaming bowl of horrendous 'food' she had prepared, and walked out of the room, heading down to the basement.

In the bathroom, Pierre turned on the water faucet.

He noticed a speck of blood on his face, and grimaced, turned on the tap, and started to wash it off.

"Pierre!" came Marta's scream from below.

Without turning the faucet off, he ran out of the bathroom, hands still dripping wet.

He crossed the hallway and into the living room, where his wife came running back up from the basement. She was pale and visibly shaken.

Marta couldn't dial the phone quickly enough, and as she spoke, her voice was a mix of fear and excitement.

"Just now," she said. " I-I was going down to feed her... Yes... It's been a few minutes now."

A hoarse voice spoke on the other end of the line: Mademoiselle, the old woman.

"Are you certain?"

Marta nodded. "Mademoiselle, as I said, I've never seen an expression like it. It's just like the photos. It's... wonderful."

The husband, meanwhile, was flicking on the television. With the remote in his hand, he was trying his best to find a channel.

The upper basement hallway.

The lower room with the metal chair.

The torture room from one end.

The torture room from the other.

Then Pierre saw Anna on the screen and dropped the remote to the floor. "Sweet Jesus," he gasped, holding his hand to his mouth.

"She's so calm," Marta continued. "Her face is like... She's not there... but she *is*. I can't explain it."

Mademoiselle was silent on the other end for a moment before asking, *"But is she alive?"*

"Yes," Marta replied, almost giddy. "She's alive, Mademoiselle, she's very much alive."

Down in the basement, Anna was in the rack.

Miles was at the far end of the room, not knowing what else he could do.

With her body flayed, dripping with blood, the rack held her upright.

Her face, however, had broken free of the clamp. Just like the butchered, beaten, and mutilated women in the photographs, she was stuck in the same expression. Peering up to the ceiling, she was not looking at anything in this existence. She was seeing something... else.

And what she stared at held her in marvel. A small, strange smile had appeared.

A white, vaporous expanse, as if created by pure light, lay ahead of the veil.

Inside an infinite number of silhouettes waited.

There was no noise here, but the silence was comforting.

Time did not exist in its light, and for a moment, it was the past, present, and future of all things.

It was neither frightening nor reassuring.

There was no welcome here, and no invitation.

. . .

A sedan drove slowly up the driveway to the house on Allée Jean Baptiste Charlemagne.

The vehicle came to a stop in front of the porch, and the driver got out to open the passenger door.

From inside, Mademoiselle got out and glanced up at the house. She was frailer than she had been the last time she came here. Her age had started to affect her more, and her steps were more unsure. With a small walking stick, she ignored the offered hand of her driver and hobbled to the front, where Marta waited for her arrival.

Maxim, meanwhile, had been told to stay in his room, so he just watched the old woman from his bedroom window.

Mademoiselle did not say a word as she walked past Marta, into the house. She went straight over to the living room, over to the sideboard, and walked down the steps.

She carried on down the corridor, past the other images of martyrs framed on the wall.

Miles waited for her as she approached the ladder to the lower basement.

Climbing down first, he made sure she followed safely.

She crossed the torture room without glancing at Miles.

All she cared about, all she wanted, was in the room ahead.

. . .

Pierre stood at the far end of the room, in front of a large plastic curtain. He waited for Mademoiselle to approach.

Motioning with her cane, she pointed to the curtain. "What's all this?"

"We need to protect her from all contaminants," he replied in a reverential tone. "She's very weak."

"Can she talk?"

He nodded. "She hasn't spoken yet, but she should be capable of it."

"And how long did it last, the look?"

"Nearly three hours," he answered. "We moved her when it stopped."

Impatiently, Mademoiselle stepped behind the curtain.

Anna was no longer on the rack and had been placed in a transparent tank filled with a viscous, translucent liquid.

A bright light was above her, casting her body's mutilation in terrible clarity.

Her condition was beyond horror. It did not cause disgust; it was too astonishing for that. With only the skin of her face having survived the skinning, she looked alien and surreal.

The body was all exposed flesh, its gleaming red mixing with the patterns of veins, arteries, muscle, and bone.

Mademoiselle leaned over the tank and stared closely at her. Unable to contain her joy, she smiled at Anna.

"Did you see it, my dear?" she asked.

Anna, with fluttering eyelids, stared at the old woman for a moment before nodding.

Mademoiselle gave an almost maternal smile at the news.

"Was it the other world?" she asked hopefully, moving in closer.

Anna nodded again, now vaguely holding onto life.

Then her mouth started to move, speaking weak, almost volumeless words.

Mademoiselle moved her ear down to Anna's lips.

Taking a wheezing breath, Anna began to mutter things that only Mademoiselle could hear.

When 2 a.m. struck, the old Belfond house was abuzz. No one had slept, aside from the boy, who was in his bed snoring.

The driveway and road outside were lined with a dozen cars, and others were still arriving.

The people were dressed in fine suits and exquisite dresses. Marta and Pierre, on the porch, welcomed their guests, and they were the youngest of the group; most others were much older by decades.

Everyone wore a serious and slightly anxious expression. They tried to hide it under polite smiles and small talk with other guests, but they were all here, feeling on a knife's edge.

One of the guests, a man with skin like old bark, hugged Pierre tightly as he arrived, laughing happily.

"You've done so well," the man said. "I can't believe it's true... *finally*."

In the living room and dining room, the furniture had been cleared to allow everyone space to mingle. Drinks and canapes were laid out on a long table, and everyone stood around mingling. It had the atmosphere of a wake and the look of a gala, all in the early morning, and everyone was waiting, anticipating.

Etienne, an austere and severe-looking man in his eighties, stood on the staircase to address this small congregation. As soon as he spoke, the murmuring stopped instantly.

"Welcome, everyone," he said. "Thank you for coming at such short notice."

"Is it true?" one woman asked, to which Etienne raised his hand to silence her.

"I can confirm that last night, in this very house, at approximately 6:15 p.m., Anna Assaoui was martyred."

A slight rustle passed through the people like an electric charge.

"I ask you to say a prayer for her. For Anna Assaoui is an exceptional being, and her name will forever be remembered and honored." He took a deep breath. "In our twenty-three years of attempts, she is only the second to have reached such a blessed stage... And the first, yes, my friends, the *first*..." His stern face broke with a smile, knowing the weight of what he was about to say.

The audience held their breath.

"...the *first* to have reported to us what she saw."

The people let their astonishment break free in gasps; some cried, as others embraced—a collective feeling of not only victory, but validation of all their efforts.

Etienne continued, calming their celebration. "Between 6:15 p.m. and 9 p.m., Anna Assaoui clearly saw what lies after... Yes, you heard that correctly. Her ecstatic state lasted two hours and forty-five minutes."

The assembly was collectively aghast at the information.

"This was not a coma, nor a near-death experience," Etienne's smile did not fade. "Her heart was beating, her brain activity was normal. What she experienced was a valid and authentic state of martyrdom... At 9:15 p.m., she left that state and returned, without any medical intervention... Then at 9:45 p.m., she spoke... At this very moment, downstairs, she is still alive. But she has ceased all communication."

The assembly stirred again. Some looked down at the floor, imagining what was below.

"Mademoiselle heard her testimony. A testimony that lasted more than *six* minutes. This testimony, my dear friends, will be shared with us momentarily. I ask you for just a little more patience. Mademoiselle is upstairs and will be joining us shortly."

The old man nodded in thanks to the people and headed up the stairs to the first floor, leaving everyone abuzz.

Walking down the hallway, Etienne felt a small spring in his old step.

He stopped outside the bathroom door and knocked lightly upon it.

"Mademoiselle," he said. "They have all arrived and are waiting for you."

Mademoiselle was at the sink, staring into the mirror.

With her headscarf removed and her glasses on the side, she held a cotton pad in her hand and was removing her makeup.

As the foundation, lipstick, and mascara came off, she looked older and frailer.

Her scalp was now virtually bald, her white hair had all gone, save for a few strings, and her wrinkles ran deeper than ever.

"Thank you, Etienne," she said, distracted in her thoughts, as she removed her clip-on earrings.

The old man hesitated at the door, unable to hide his impatience. He leaned closer and spoke quietly.

"So there *was* something?" he asked.

After a pause, her monotone reply came. *"There was."*

Etienne clasped his hands together with joy. "And... it was clear?"

"Crystal."

"No vagueness?"

"It allowed no room for interpretation, Etienne."

The old man closed his eyes, relieved, overcome by the news.

"Thank you, Mademoiselle. Thank you." He looked upward with a grateful smile.

With her makeup and all refinery removed, Mademoiselle sat down on the edge of the bathtub. Picking up her handbag, she opened it and rifled through it.

She pulled out an old photograph.

There she was, in her thirties. Before the failed marriages. Before the cancer. Before the weight of the cause overtook her life. Before her body became what it is now.

She peered up into the mirror again.

She knew she was once a great beauty, but now she saw herself as a sexless relic.

"Etienne?" she called out hopefully.

Outside, a shuffling of feet as Etienne returned to the door.

"*Yes, mademoiselle?*""

She put the photograph back into her handbag and, from inside, took out a small-caliber revolver.

"Can you imagine what there is after death?" she asked sadly..

"Are you all right?" Etienne asked, looking surprised. "Mademoiselle?

"Well, can you?" she asked again, as a tear ran down her cheek.

From the other side of the door, Etienne's worry was evident. "*No, Mademoiselle, I...*"

She closed her eyes. "Well, please, Etienne, keep doubting."

She slid the barrel of the revolver between her lips.

"*Mademois—*"

The gunshot rang throughout the house, echoing around the rooms like a tolling bell.

In the lower basement was Anna. Now lying on white linen, her whole body had been bandaged, and she was connected to half a dozen monitors, a drip, and machines. An oxygen mask covered her mouth, assisting her weakened breathing.

Her eyes were half closed, as she gently whispered to herself, "Lucie... Lucie... Lucie."

The monitor sounded the beeping of her heartbeat.

Slower and slower it went, as her eyes opened and looked upward.

"Lucie..."

A rattle in her lungs broke her breath, as her heartbeat slowed to a halt.

"Lu..."

The monitor let out its continuous tone as her breathing stopped, taking her voice with it.

Her eyes remained open as she stared, and her pupils dilated.

Then a small smile crept over her face.

Martyr
from Greek μάρτυς, g
en. μάρτυρος
"witness"